MATTHEW'S HAND

Books by Charles Larson:

MATTHEW'S HAND
SOMEONE'S DEATH
THE CHINESE GAME

MATTHEW'S HAND

CHARLES LARSON

DOUBLEDAY & COMPANY, INC.

GARDEN CITY, NEW YORK

1974

*This one is for Wyn and
the ship's library.*

All of the characters in this book are fictitious, and any resemblance to actual
persons, living or dead, is purely coincidental.

Library of Congress Cataloging in Publication Data

Larson, Charles.
Matthew's hand.

I. Title.
PZ4.L3357Mat [PS3562.A75]   813'.5'4
ISBN 0-385-05184-0
Library of Congress Catalog Card Number 74-5528

First Edition

PROLOGUE

Nothing in the canyon was older than he was, except the rock he was stretched across.

He was older than the burned underbrush and the stunted trees gripping the bluffs above him.

Once he had watched a blind fox drown in three inches of stagnant marsh water six inches from his leathery nose, and as old as the fox had been, he was more than six times older than that.

He had come here in October 1881, fourteen months after toppling off a boat in a California harbor; he had survived drought and fire and earthquakes too numerous to mention; he had seen everything he cared to see, and he had thought everything worth thinking.

Now, dreamy and deaf, he spent his days packed like a fist inside his shell, soaking up the sun at the edge of the pond, letting the wind blow him his food. He was particularly partial to a little red berry the birds sometimes dropped, and when one of these landed near him, he would greedily inch out his reptilian neck, further and further, shaking with passion, until he had salvaged it.

This was the vulgar position he found himself in early one March afternoon when a sack came tumbling down the cliff to splash into the water beside his rock.

In his heyday, of course, a lesser stir would have sprung him back upon himself like a touched anemone; now, nothing worked. His two port legs swam foolishly; the hind starboard one tried to lock against a tail that was still extended straight aft in a vain effort to counterbalance the exposed head.

He appeared as ridiculous as he felt, and if anything alive had made the splash, he would have been slaughtered in his tracks.

But none of the objects in the sack had been alive for days.

Above him, an engine coughed; tires spun gravel down the hill and he folded his wrinkled throat in chagrin under his carapace, far too long after the fact, shaken and berryless.

Gradually the ripples and the gravel and the sounds of the car diminished and died. The air cooled. He slept and dreamed of crazy dangers, and tried to think, when he awoke, what was different about the canyon now, and decided that it must be the sack. He noticed that it had split across the top and by craning his neck he could see into it, and what he saw was a brown-haired severed human head lying on its right cheek, looking past him out of reproachful eyes, and two severed white hands that trailed stubby fingers languidly through the green water.

It was meaningless. It was nothing to fear and nothing to eat.

It was part of the landscape, like him—though not as old.

The wind had risen; the clouds had begun to boil in the east.

That night there would be a terrible storm.

CHAPTER ONE

When the telephone rang, Jesus Mary was under the counter somewhere, searching for a dime he'd dropped, and Gloria had just gone
into the kitchen, so Isabel slammed down her coffee cup and grabbed
the receiver herself.

"All right, you sick son of a bitch," she said, "now you're in trouble. There's a cop on the extension and he's already started a trace,
and when he gets you he's going to put you in jail for twenty goddamn
years, how would you like that?"

"Wouldn't like that a little bit," Sanderson said.

"Who *is* this?" Isabel demanded.

"Me," Sanderson said. "David."

"Hang on a second, sweetheart," Isabel said. She pressed the
phone against her bosom and said in Spanish: "Uncle Jesus Mary,
will you please calm down, for God's sake? It's David. David."

"Who?" Jesus Mary shouted. He was a big Indian from Nayarit,
below Mazatlan, emotional like all those coast people, perhaps more
than emotional since the attacks had started, perhaps a little para-
noid. Every visible inch of him seemed to be either tattooed or
scarred. He'd done some picing on the Northern Circuit, he'd been
a fair fighter in his twenties, light-heavyweight, he'd worked the tuna
boats, he'd even dived for a couple of seasons off the tourist rocks
in Acapulco. He was *macho* from top to bottom, Isabel thought, and
uncle or not, fifty or not, tattooed or not, he could still scare her half
to death when he paraded around like the head bull in the barnyard.

"Give me the phone, *chica*," he said.

"I'm talking. It's David."

So he took the phone away from her. "David?" he said. "This is
Chu-Chu."

Sulkily Isabel poured sugar substitute into her coffee and watched
the storm flail the cafe window. The darkness, the noise, the infre-
quent creeping headlights mirrored in the flooded oceanfront street

made her feel more bereft than ever. She could imagine Sanderson stretched in his elegant way along the oyster-colored sofa in their Pasadena apartment, probably with an inelegant beer in one hand and his unlighted pipe on his chest, while the rain pecked genteelly at the mullioned windows. Here at the beach, fifty miles from home, the rain flapped in from the sea like a loose blind, black and loud and cold as ship's canvas. At her feet, Jesus Mary's poodle, Harpo, quivered every time the thunder crashed. He was a big cowardly standard, about as smart as your average chicken. Once Isabel had drawn a line in the dust and put his stupid nose to it to test him, and sure enough, there he had sat for hours, cross-eyed and hypnotized. Or at least that had been her story, although Jesus Mary, who loved the old dog, hadn't bought it, claiming that Harpo often grew lethargic after a big meal and had probably just been sitting there digesting and thinking. Derisively, Isabel had said that Harpo couldn't think his way out of his own doghouse alone, but when Jesus Mary's eyes grew flinty, she changed the subject.

". . . oh, no, the same old crap," Jesus Mary was saying. "Who ever heard of a bigot with imagination? They write, they phone, break windows, ask me why I don't go back to Russia. I say I've never *been* to Russia, but when I get my final papers and take over the government, I'll send *them* to Russia."

A measured double thump from upstairs shook the ceiling light fixture, and Jesus Mary said: "David, wait a minute, it's my wife," and shouted, in Spanish, at the ceiling: "Yes, all right, we hear you, don't break the damned cane!"

"I'll get it," Isabel said.

"Here, say goodbye first," Jesus Mary growled and handed her the phone.

"Hi, sweetheart, goodbye," Isabel said. "Judy thumped. She probably wants to go to the bathroom. Mrs. Billroth's up there with her, but sometimes she can't lift her alone. Do you miss me?"

"Does the ocean miss the shore?" Sanderson asked. "Does the desert miss the rain? Does the exile miss his homeland? Does the porter miss his train?"

"Does the porter miss—"

"It's the technique I expect you to admire," Sanderson said, "not the substance."

"Ah," Isabel said. "Well, I *do*. I mean, how many other girls are lucky enough to have a writer for a pal?"

"That's it exactly," Sanderson said.

"So how's the new script coming?"

"Coming fine."

"Did anybody at the studio notice I was gone today?"

"Everybody noticed. They all wanted to know whatever had become of that interesting little actress who always missed her mark."

Forlornly, Isabel said: "I really think I should have come to work, David."

"What for?"

"Well, they had to rearrange the whole shooting schedule, everything. Kapralos just raised hell when I called."

"Screw Kapralos," Sanderson said. "Production managers always raise hell. They're paid to raise hell. You've earned a day off. You're a star now. Use your clout."

"*I'm* a star?"

"To me you're a star," Sanderson said.

"Then who's the joker," Isabel asked, "who keeps putting my name at the end of the credit-crawl just above the bit players?"

"Wait until you win your Emmy and see where they put your name."

"Why aren't *you* producing this series?" Isabel asked.

"Blixen feels the same way."

"Sure. Did you see Friday's dailies?"

"Yes."

"Well?"

"Well, what? You were splendid."

"I didn't feel splendid," Isabel said. "I just couldn't reach down for it, you know? Everything was on the surface. . . . What did Blixen say?"

"Liked it."

"David, come on."

The line hummed emptily for a moment. Then Sanderson said: "He thought you were a little surface."

"Maybe I'm just not the actress I'm cracked up to be," Isabel muttered.

"Quit it, Isabel."

"If I was, I don't think I'd let my private worries affect my work like that."

"Let me tell you about actors," Sanderson said. "I love actors. My mother and father were actors. I've been around actors all my life.

And I have never known one—not *one*—who really believed that the show had to go on. That's what understudies are for."

"There aren't any understudies in TV," Isabel said. "Just permanent replacements."

"Nobody replaces talent, babe."

Isabel rested her chin moodily on the heel of her free hand. "It's just that I feel so sorry for these people, David. They do need me."

"I know."

"Judy's sick anyhow—she shouldn't have to go through this."

"What does the doctor say?"

"Same old thing. Sacroiliac. She gets nervous and the muscles tighten up. We don't tell her half the things that happen."

"Like what?"

"Oh—red paint on the door, a dead rat wrapped in a Mexican flag on the back porch—"

"In a Mexican *flag?*"

"Well, you've got your anti-Communist nuts down here, and then you've got your anti-Mexican nuts."

"I think Jesus ought to call in the police."

"I think he ought to call in the National *Guard*. But you know Jesus. He bought a restaurant and if he bought a problem along with it, good, he likes problems. He'd let the place burn down around his ears before he'd ask a cop for help. He's got his daughter in the kitchen and his wife in the bedroom and that's enough for him."

"What about his niece?"

"Yeah, he's got me, too, I guess," Isabel said.

"You'll be staying a while longer then?"

"Should I?"

"Up to you, babe."

"I can't stay forever. Saturday, Sunday, Monday, it's been three days—"

"Are you worried about Kapralos?"

"I kind of am."

"Don't be."

"He said he couldn't possibly change the schedule again."

"He'd change it quick enough if you were in the hospital."

"He said no."

"How long would you *like* to stay?"

"Well . . . maybe through tomorrow? Gloria does all the cooking, but I've been helping Jesus out on the tables—"

"So he has some customers."

"Oh, sure. Friends. Antibigots . . ."

"All right," Sanderson said, "I'll write you out of tomorrow's scenes then."

"Would it be a lot of work?"

"Actually, no. Not for Super Story Editor."

It was the way he said "actually." It reminded her of the hair at the back of his neck, and of his narrow English feet, and somehow of one of his pipes in particular, a clay Churchwarden that usually rested next to his typewriter when ideas wouldn't come. He hadn't smoked in years, but he needed the pipes, he said, to bite down on, like bullets, from time to time. "David," she began.

"Yes. What?"

"Nothing."

"Are you crying?"

"No."

"Ah, babe—don't cry."

"You seem so far away."

"I'm as close as the phone."

"That's not close enough."

Behind her the front door squealed open, and she spun toward it so fast (thinking *firebomb? grenade?*) that she nearly hurled herself off her stool, but it was only Jesus Mary, in the middle of one of his hot flashes, going out to stand in the rain and breathe the raw wind for a while. He was always too warm. He had spent a lifetime among chilled women in sweltering rooms and he pretended to believe that this had somehow weakened his lungs. He said that both his parents had lived to be ninety, but that he himself hadn't the chance of a snowflake in hell of equaling that record, parboiled as he had been by women. Lightning picked him out theatrically; thunder spilled along the soaked black bluffs behind his besieged restaurant; his dog quivered and moaned against Isabel's ankles. "David, listen, I have to go," she said. "Judy'll burst."

"I'll call you tomorrow."

"Yes, I love you."

"I love you, too, babe. Good night."

"Good night."

She hung up and rested her face in her hands, amazed at herself for breaking off the conversation, irritated at David for allowing her to, furious with Judy for thumping and with Gloria for never hearing her thump, and especially with Jesus Mary for getting them all into this grotesque mess in the first place. Meanwhile, that beribboned wreck, Harpo, had staggered across the room to his empty pan and was rasping his tongue, like a file, across its dry bottom.

"Here, dummy, here," Isabel said. She poured a little coffee into her saucer and set it on the floor at her feet. *"Here."*

Harpo came staggering back, panting thirstily at her, and Isabel thought, oh, what the hell, and put down the cup, too. She watched Mr. Graceful step in the saucer and get his ear in the cup and spill about nine times more than he was able to down, but he seemed satisfied at last, so she sighed and went to look after Judy, shaking her head.

At the back of the place, she and Gloria pushed for a simultaneous few seconds on opposite sides of the swinging kitchen door, until Gloria saw who it was through the little window and gave way. Gloria was twenty-five, two years older than Isabel, but even as children—as cousins and next-door neighbors in both Nayarit and Texas—Isabel had been the dominant one, the leader, the first to sneak smokes and keep a diary, to fall in love. Placid and puzzled, Gloria had always tried everything a little too late, when Judy, her mom—warned by Isabel's mother—was already on the lookout for cigarette breath and moony eyes. She had inherited her father's classic Indian bones and Judy's North American temperament, an unsettling combination to most men, though she had somehow acquired a Portuguese *novio* named Cabral, a butcher who had been on strike for seven months and who spent most of his time in Jesus Mary's kitchen, thoughtfully eating cold tacos and untying Gloria's apron whenever she walked by. Laughing, Gloria stepped back to let Isabel in. "I'm sorry," she said. "I didn't notice you out there."

"Jude thumped," Isabel said.

"Oh, did she?"

"No problem, I'm on my way," Isabel said. She swept past Cabral, who was tilted back in his chair by the stove and who pleasantly waved his taco at her when she said hi to him. He was a curly-haired, thickset man of thirty with a sweet, countertenor voice and no apparent ambition whatsoever. Jesus Mary loathed him and implied that anybody who could sing that high must have had a terrible accident sometime. He said he'd seen some farfetched love affairs, but that this one took the cake, and he was continually pressing Sanderson to introduce Gloria to some of *his* friends. He was very fond of

Sanderson and told everyone how proud he was of Isabel for hooking a winner like that.

Winner, Isabel thought as she climbed the dark back stairs. David had seemed like anything but a winner when she had first run into him. They had met at the start of the current TV season in Nils Blixen's office and had taken an irrational dislike to each other at once. Isabel, hired to play a Chicana secretary in Blixen's new series, *Stagg at Bay,* had rewritten most of Sanderson's lines after one reading, and had further endeared herself to the man by cornering him in the studio commissary and telling him that he didn't know enough about Chicano word rhythms to stick up his nose. In addition, she had eaten all his potato chips. (He learned eventually never to fight with her at mealtimes; battle stimulated her hypothalamus.) At three o'clock, the assistant director had found them in Sanderson's office, still fighting, and had carried Isabel off to the stage, where all afternoon she had caught glimpses of Sanderson prowling around behind the camera, gnashing his big teeth and listening to her word rhythms.

She truly had not liked him. She had thought him arrogant and inhibited, full of Anglo preconceptions, an insufferable snob. He had said that on the contrary, *she* was the snob, *she* had the preconceptions, she appeared to believe that one had to be born to ethnic values in order to write about them. He said he had run into her kind before, all mouth and a yard wide. He called her a Stone Age liberal and declared that if he had signed his work Sanchez instead of Sanderson she would have been touting him for a Brown Power award by now.

"My God," she had shouted to Judy over the phone that particular night, "how I detest that vicious bonehead, *tia!* I *detest* him! Can you imagine any man talking to me like that?"

"You know who he sounds a little like?" Judy had asked in her vague, blond way.

"He sounds like Spiro T. Agnew, for Christ's sake," Isabel had shouted. "That's who he sounds like!"

"No. Well, yes, but somebody else."

"Attila the Hun!"

"Chu-Chu," Judy had said.

Isabel, trying to add a little water to her bourbon at the drainboard, had jumped and spilled half her drink over herself. *"Chu-Chu! Jesus Mary? Our Jesus?"*

"Don't you think so?"

"No!"

"Think about it."

"I don't have to think about it! One's a raving male chauvinist, the other's—" Isabel had stopped. "Tia, come to the party! This puling child—"

"You hate him clear to your fingertips."

"Further! I can't *express* to you—"

"Neither could I," her aunt had said reminiscently, "the first time Chu-Chu wouldn't let me win a fight. I was a secretary from Ohio, on vacation, and Chu-Chu was organizing the dock workers in Mazatlan. Ah, chica, chica, what crazy days those were."

"Jude, it doesn't have anything to do with winning fights!" But it did, partly, and Isabel knew it, and that drab knowledge was what shook her the most. That was the trouble with Judy. It wasn't fair for someone who looked so much like a blue-eyed horse to be so knowledgeable about the heart.

"I suppose he likes Mexican food," Judy had said, half to herself. "I never knew a man who didn't. You're not a bad cook. Why don't you make him some enchiladas, couple of—"

"Are you out of your *bird?*" Isabel had screamed. "I *hate* the bastard! Why should I feed him?"

"It always worked when I fed Chu-Chu."

"I don't *want* anything to work! Work? Work? What are you talking about!"

"I don't know," Judy had answered, and gone on to discuss her ailments, which as always were vivid and excruciating.

But of course the damage had been done. If a little knowledge was a dangerous thing, a little insight, Isabel discovered, could be catastrophic. She had continued to glare and bridle at Sanderson, but the truth was that he was the only man she had ever known, except Chu-Chu, who was more interesting to her than reading. She had brooded about this for a while, and then had thrown a buffet dinner party for the cast and some of the production people on the occasion of *Stagg*'s air-debut in September, and against her every instinct, she had invited Sanderson. He had been startled, but he'd come, and more than that, he'd eaten so many enchiladas that she had run out and been embarrassed before her peers. He said her brain reminded him of a flicker's nest, but that he was a slave to her enchiladas. Someday, he said, he would try to teach her how to cook a decent relleno as well, and to fry chorizos properly, and, to her incredulous horror, she had socked him in the mouth and run hysterically into her bedroom, where she had thrown up and gotten one of her blind migraines and thought seriously of suicide. She'd heard her guests murmuring in the living room and then gaily calling goodnight to one another, but she hadn't unlocked her door to any of them.

Toward four in the morning, the automatic dishwasher wakened her. She peered out to see Sanderson seated in front of the TV set, watching a movie and drinking beer. He had cleaned the whole place, put the food away, fed the cat, everything. She had muttered: "Oh, Christ, what's the use," wearily, and then let him make love to her on the daybed on the screened-in porch for almost an hour and a half, until dawn, and had enjoyed herself so much that she thought her knees were going to come unhooked. Two weeks later she had moved into Sanderson's Pasadena apartment as if it were the most natural thing in the world. Everybody around there had called her Mrs. Sanderson until she had printed MS CHAVEZ in big block letters under David's name on the hall mailbox, and that had fixed that. . . .

At the top of the stairs she paused to close a dormer window some-one had left a little open and to stare out at the sheets of rain that battered the roof. Mud from the thinly planted slope had begun to inch over the low retaining wall and advance like lava upon the garage and the old shed Jesus Mary used for a storehouse. When the last trump sounded, Isabel thought, this is how the senile earth will look, heaving over the restless dead, lit like a Max Reinhardt pro-duction. . . . Nauseous, she nearly crossed herself. And it was then —while she was pondering unquiet corpses and retribution and blas-phemous girls who strayed from the true church—that something touched her gently on the nape of the neck.

She didn't scream; she was incapable of screaming. She was seized with the outlandish conceit that all her blood had drained straight down to her ankles and that if she were to topple over, she'd bob right back up again, like a weighted doll. *I can't turn,* she thought, and then: *No, I've got to turn,* and then: *No, I can't possibly turn.* She counted to three and said serenely: "Yes?"

"Gloria?" Mrs. Billroth whispered.

"Hm?" Isabel asked.

"Oh, is it Isabel?" muttered Mrs. Billroth. "We thumped. I ex-pected Gloria to—"

"No, it's Isabel," Isabel said. She cranked her head around and gave the chunky figure behind her a dazzling smile. "Hi," she said.

"Hi," said Mrs. Billroth. "Did I scare you?"

"No, no," Isabel said.

"I thought you jumped a little there," said Mrs. Billroth.

Lightning jiggled along the bluff; thunder shook the hallway. In the livid flash, Mrs. Billroth squinted nervously past Isabel out the streaming window into the backyard. She was a short woman who cut her iron-gray hair straight across the tops of her ears, like a Saxon serf. There were some people, Isabel had come to realize, who were so breathtakingly ill-favored as to somehow have gone clear around the circle and rereached beauty. Indeed, she had once described Mrs. Billroth to Sanderson as beautiful, only to have Sanderson say, after he had met her, that he was surprised at Isabel's cruelty. Baffled and hurt, Isabel had insisted: "But she *is* beautiful, David! What's the matter with you? Can't you see it?"

"She looks," Sanderson had said, "like a pockmarked frog."

"Okay, yes," Isabel had answered. "But that doesn't—"

"Dear one, listen—"

"David, David," Isabel had said, "do you remember Marie Dressler?"

"Certainly I remember Marie Dressler."

"Describe Marie Dressler to me."

Sanderson had measured her for a long moment and then said: "No."

"Boy, you're a poor loser," Isabel had said.

"I know that," Sanderson had said. "I've never claimed otherwise." And he had gone back to his work, the picture of dignity.

But at least it had served to clarify the matter in Isabel's mind. Marie Dressler had been an interior beauty, a loving grotesque, and so was Mrs. Billroth, and that was what everyone responded to. Jesus Mary had certainly responded to it when he had first driven through Oceanport and seen the FOR SALE sign on the forlorn Tea Shoppe and gone in to check it out. He said Mrs. Billroth had been so severe and motherly that he had capitulated to her tough sale terms before he knew what he was doing, which was untrue but graceful—or at least about as graceful as Jesus Mary ever got. The fact was that Mrs. Billroth had been more or less on the ropes financially for years, and was ripe for the plucking. Jesus Mary had picked up a good bargain, and knew it. He had also picked up a firm friend, and he knew that. Before they ever approached a deal, Mrs. Billroth had laid the neighborhood's problem right on the line. She had pointed out the lack of Spanish and Oriental surnames on the shop windows, the absence of black faces on the street. Most of her neighbors, she'd said, considered Richard M. Nixon a pinko egghead dupe and couldn't conceive of a sounder presidential ticket than Goldwater-Reagan. Laughing, Jesus Mary had told her not to fret about him; he said he'd been a Mexican in Texas and that there weren't a whole hell of a lot of rungs lower than that, but Mrs. Billroth had warned him not to bet on it; he was standing on one right now, she'd said.

So, anyway, Jesus Mary had been warned.

Even then everything might have worked out if he hadn't set off some firecrackers and played a number of patriotic marches on his hi-fi the day the Vietnam War ended. The neighbor on his right, a hardware merchant named Junkin, came over in a friendly way to tell him that that was kind of a dumb thing to do because somebody might think he was a Commie, and Jesus Mary said, well, there was certainly a coincidence for you because he *was* a Commie. Junkin turned white as a sheet and was never quite the same man after that.

Fifteen minutes later Jesus Mary's cook and both waitresses quit and by suppertime the phone calls had started. Gloria, who had been working at Bullock's in downtown L.A., was the first ally to show up. Mrs. Billroth was the second.

"I suppose you came over to say I told you so," Jesus Mary said.

"No," said Mrs. Billroth, "to wait table."

And that's what she had done, parading back and forth from the kitchen and nodding hello to the old friends who dropped by to tell her that she was making a bloody ass of herself.

"You better go on home," Jesus Mary said, "you'll end up as isolated as we are."

"Well, we'll burn that bridge when we come to it," said Mrs. Billroth.

In point of fact, not all of Mrs. Billroth's friends condemned her. One or two—like the town G.P., a man named Trout, and a young minister called Brouwer—took the opposite tack and actually began patronizing Jesus Mary's place, always sitting ostentatiously at the window table and leaving extravagant tips. But even their presence hadn't made much of a dent in the paint-throwing and the dirty phone calls. For one thing, Brouwer was too new to the town and Dr. Trout was probably too eccentric, and for another both of them had developed acid stomachs from all of the unaccustomed chili, and hadn't been dropping by as often lately, particularly since Judy had collapsed and Gloria had had to replace her in the kitchen.

Nevertheless their hearts were in the right place, Isabel thought with a sudden rush of tenderness, and so was Mrs. Billroth's, and that was what counted.

"Enid," she said impulsively, "I adore you, did I ever tell you that?" And she grasped Mrs. Billroth and planted a big kiss right between her tiny eyes.

"Good *grief*," Mrs. Billroth said, struggling.

"Oh, you're not hurt and you know it," Isabel said. "If you want to talk about pain, let's talk about poor swollen Judy."

"Why? Judith's all right," Mrs. Billroth said. She continued to puff and poke at her hair, but Isabel noticed that she didn't try to rub away the kiss. "Don't you worry about Judith," she said.

"Don't tell me you got her to use the *bed*pan!" Isabel exclaimed.

"Oh, the *thump!*" Mrs. Billroth said. "No, no, *I* thumped. We wanted to know what all the racket was about. Out in the backyard . . ."

"What racket? When?"

"Why, you must have heard it, it almost scared the two of us out of our wits."

"I was on the phone," Isabel said, "but Jesus Mary didn't say anything. Gloria and Cabral were in the kitchen and apparently they didn't hear it. What did it sound like?"

"Firecrackers," Mrs. Billroth said.

"Oh, it did not," Judy moaned from her doorway.

Lightning illuminated the stuffy hall just as Isabel and Mrs. Billroth turned, and Judy blinked like a blinded soubrette and gripped the lintel until her fingers were white while the follow-up thunder cracked over the bluffs. She was gray-faced and haggard, clearly in pain; her bare feet under the long, pink, lace-edged nightgown broke Isabel's heart. "Tia!" she snapped. "For Pete's sake, what are you doing out of bed?"

"It was a door banging," Judy gasped.

"You get on one side of her, I'll get on the other," commanded Mrs. Billroth. "Hook her arm around your neck there."

"Let go of the jamb, tia!" Isabel said.

"Alley-oop," Mrs. Billroth grunted.

Hissing contradictory orders, panting, Isabel and Mrs. Billroth hauled Judy, between them, like a wet sandbag, back to the rumpled bed and inserted her under the covers in sections, head and shoulders first, rigid waist next, finally the feet. Then they discovered that she was on her stomach, a position she couldn't abide, but Judy warned them that if they so much as breathed on her again she'd call the Mafia and have them tortured. Mrs. Billroth decided that that was good enough for her, but Isabel said she scorned the threat because everybody in TV and motion pictures knew there was no Mafia, just ask Al Ruddy. Who was Al Ruddy? Mrs. Billroth wanted to know, so Isabel had to tell her that Al Ruddy was the brave man who produced *The Godfather,* and how the Mafia had told *him* there was no Mafia and had insisted that he never use the terrible word in his picture, which he had not. Mrs. Billroth pivoted a full ninety degrees to study her, unblinkingly, and Isabel said: "Cross my heart and hope to die, Enid, that's what happened," and Mrs. Billroth muttered something about cloud cuckoo-land, and went downstairs to get Judith one of her special pain pills.

Sympathetically Isabel picked up the heavy blackthorn cane and stood it against the wall, then squatted between her aunt and the door to adjust the little bedside lamp so that it wouldn't shine in Judy's eyes. Judy managed a ghost of a smile and whispered either gracias or thanks, and tried to brush the sweat out of her hairline.

"Tia?" Isabel asked. "Would you like a little something to go with the pill? Little snort?"

"Uh-uh. It's better."

"Sure?"

"It's that banging that worries me."

"Are you positive you didn't dream it? None of the rest of us heard anything."

"What if it's some nut in the garage?"

"No, the garage is closed and locked. I could see it from the stair window. Maybe it was a car backfiring. Enid thought it was firecrackers."

"No, she didn't," Judy said. "She knows what it was. We both heard it. She was the one who said it was a door in the first place, but then when I wanted to get up and check, she said no, it must have just been some kids playing around. . . . Isabel—go see."

"My God, Jude, it's raining cats and dogs out there!"

"What if they try to set us on fire?"

"Tia . . ."

Two enormous tears slid down the slick, horselike nose, and Isabel slapped her rounded knees and hoisted herself to her feet. "Right," she said, thinking, well, what the hell, maybe I can con Jesus Mary into it. She touched her fingers lightly against her aunt's waxen forehead. "I'll be back in a minute. You take your pill like a good girl when Enid brings it, okay?"

"Okay."

Isabel fooled a little bit with the covers around Judy's neck, then tiptoed out into the hot, low hallway. The rain was drumming as noisily as ever on the roof, but someone had turned on the stair light, which took away a good deal of the Frankenstein menace. Just to play it safe, Isabel peeped out the dormer window at the garage below, and, yes, the door was plainly locked. Women, she thought irritably, my God, what are we, so starved for drama that we have to invent monsters to populate every two-bit storm that comes along? Outside, the wind screamed; thunder cracked like a redwood falling. All right, all right, Isabel amended, *four-bit,* and got to snuffling and chuckling so at her own wit that she nearly knocked into Mrs. Billroth before she noticed her slumped halfway down the stairs.

Mrs. Billroth, whiter than Judy had been, was staring off at nothing, one hand gripping her chest.

Bending over, Isabel said: "Enid? Why, honey, what's the matter? Are you sick?"

Mutely Mrs. Billroth nodded.

"Hey, listen," Isabel said. "It's only a rainstorm. It'll end. Everything ends."

"Harpo's gone," said Mrs. Billroth.

After a second, Isabel said: "Gone—where? I don't understand. Gone out? In the rain? Is he lost?"

"No," said Mrs. Billroth. "He's in Jesus Mary's lap." The exhausted, ugly face crumpled like a child's. "They've poisoned *Harpo,*" Mrs. Billroth said.

CHAPTER TWO

"Mr. Blixen?" murmured the black maid. "It's for you, telephone."

Blixen, caught with a drink in each hand and a curried shrimp in his mouth, mutely lifted his surprised eyebrows.

"Well, good God," Norm Seacliff said, "I can accept you Hollywood types having yourselves paged at Chasen's, but I'd always understood that private parties were sacred out here."

"Nothing's sacred out here," Art Todd said. He was the host, the only man on the terrace over forty without a tie. The air was wet and cold, but the body of the storm had lost itself far to the west, now, over the ocean, and already the rich, hidden canyons beyond Sunset were stirring into outdoor-lighted life. Someone had begun to play the piano in Todd's living room—Vernon Duke songs, sad, dated and lovely; groups of guests chatted in his shipshape den and his formal dining room and shot pool downstairs on a table made in 1892.

"Sheila," Seacliff said, "the man can't hold this pose of doglike devotion forever. He has a telephone call to take."

"Oh!" Mrs. Seacliff said and turned blankly. She was a slender, black-haired young woman in a green sheath, a New Yorker, like her husband, ill at ease around barbecue pits. She'd been talking earnestly to Murphy Smith, who played the broken-nosed private detective, Saul Stagg, in *Stagg at Bay* and who was a New Yorker himself and always gave her a brief handshake instead of a kiss and called her Mrs. Seacliff when they met. Blixen beamed at her behind the shrimp in his mouth and dipped one of the glasses in a little salute. "Oh, you brought my *drink,*" Mrs. Seacliff said.

"Your scotch and Fresca," said her husband.

"I don't know why you all wince at that," Sheila said. "I can't see why it's any worse than rum and Coca-Cola."

"*I* didn't wince," Murf Smith said. "May I?"

"Oh, certainly—here," Sheila said. "Try it."

"My second wife," Todd rumbled, "got on a Courvoisier and Ripple kick once."

"That sounds good," Sheila said.

Murf said: "Um, delicious," and stole another sip of Mrs. Seacliff's drink before handing it back.

"I killed her," Todd said. He pointed the stump of his cigar toward a shadowed arbor. "I caught her near the roses with that abomination in her hand and I pinched her head off."

"Is that when they made you studio chief, Art?" Seacliff asked.

"Around there," Todd said. "They told me they were looking for somebody with taste and strength."

Seacliff laughed, so Murf laughed, too, because Seacliff was even bigger than Todd, president of the network, although Murphy stopped the moment Mrs. Seacliff glanced at him. "Can I get you a shrimp, Mrs. Seacliff?" he asked.

"Please," Sheila said.

Breathing apologies, Murf eased past the black maid, who was waiting to show Blixen the way to the telephone, and Blixen nodded at her to indicate that he was ready now, and put down his drink on a nearby glass-topped table. "Excuse me, Sheila."

"Nils—just a minute," Todd said, "who knows you're here?"

"I didn't think anyone did."

"Did they say who it was, Pauline?" Todd asked.

"No, sir," said the maid. "Just wondered if Mr. Blixen was around, and I said yes. Some man."

"Get his name, please, will you? Always get his name."

"Yes, sir," Pauline said, and left.

"This is supposed to be a party, after all," Todd complained. "We have gathered here to suck up to Norman Seacliff, have we not?"

"Yes, we have," Blixen said.

"And I am not about to spend Lord alone knows how much money on alcohol and starlets and all that only to have my sickest show's producer slip away before the fish is hooked."

"Well, I don't blame you," Seacliff said.

"You could save us all a great deal of time and grief, you know, Norman," Blixen said, "if you'd just tell us frankly that you're picking up *Stagg* next week."

"No question about it," Seacliff said.

"That you're picking up *Stagg*?"

"That I could save you a great deal of time and grief."

Wearily Mrs. Seacliff said: "Someday I'm going to come to a California party and somebody'll talk about something other than business and the shock'll kill me."

"By the same token," Seacliff said, "I could give my associates corporate heart failure by reaching a decision without consulting them, couldn't I?"

"Is anybody cold?" Mrs. Seacliff asked. "I wonder if I ought to have my wrap."

"Norman," Todd said, "*Stagg at Bay* has shown more power against those ball-crackin' movies than any series the network has put in that time slot in the last three years."

"You were the one who said it was sick, not me," Seacliff said.

"There's nothing sick about a twenty-eight share against *Love Story*," Blixen said.

"Except that you have to ask yourself how many times *Love Story*'s been rerun."

"Norman," Blixen began.

"Look, look," Seacliff said, laughing, "I like the show, I always have. I like the concept, I like Murphy, I like the girl."

"Do you realize," Todd said, "that that inexperienced child pulls more fan mail now than Murphy does?" He looked at Blixen. "Doesn't she? Somebody told me that."

"Half again as much," Blixen said. "Isabel's an asset already, in her first season—she's going to be a tremendous star someday."

"Nils," Seacliff said, "you're preaching to a convert. You don't have to twist my arm. I like her. I like the fellow who plays the minister—"

"Gould."

"Gould, all of them. You've got a very strong TV family there, immensely strong. As a matter of fact, I think that's your brightest asset, your people. If you can keep the group together, keep the chemistry going, well . . ." He shrugged.

"Strong people in strong stories," Todd said.

"That's what sells the product," Seacliff said. He teetered back and forth on his polished toes, brushed a bug away from his polished scalp. "Character stories," he said.

Blixen, swallowing the last of his gin and tonic, felt, rather than heard, the shift in Seacliff's voice—the casual lack of emphasis, the magician's practiced misdirection. Todd, who evidently hadn't heard anything of the sort, was trying to change the subject when Blixen said: "Norman—excuse me just a second," and Todd was so astounded by the interruption that he closed his mouth at once and stood gaping at Blixen as though the other had lost his mind. "What exactly do you mean," Blixen went on, "by 'character stories'?"

"By what?" Seacliff asked vaguely.

"Character stories as opposed to what other kind, for instance."

"What other kind," Todd exclaimed. "Are you cuckoo? There isn't any other kind. He's talking about *character* stories—the kind of stories you've done all season—tight, strong, actionful."

"Well, actionful within reason," Seacliff said.

"Of course," Todd said, but almost before the words were out his stance had changed, his entire bearing; he hunched forward now, his hands in his jacket pockets, thumbs out, like a captain on his bridge in a storm, alert from skull to soles. "Yes . . . yes," he said slowly. "Within reason."

"Actionful but not violent," Blixen suggested, and Seacliff raised his shoulders and inclined his head to one side like an Italian vegetable peddler, as though to say "There you are, now why couldn't *I* have thought of those words?"

"Funny," Todd began in a tired, older tone, "I thought TV violence was last year's headline."

"In America's heartland, Arthur," Blixen said, "TV violence is every year's headline."

"When am I going to learn that?" Todd asked, and bit off the end of a fresh cigar. "So who the hell is it this time?"

"Who's what this time?" Seacliff countered.

"Come on, Norman," Blixen said, "you're a continent away. The FCC can't hear you."

Seacliff smiled and then dug the heels of his hands into his eye sockets. "Ah, God," he sighed, "how I wish I'd gone to work for the telephone company the way my mom wanted me to." He continued to rub his eyes for a while longer, and then he said: "It's a congressman named Connaught."

"Never heard of him," Todd said.

"You will," Seacliff said. "The hearings started last week. I'll probably be called in April. I understand *Time*'s already planning a cover story on him. He claims that all the sex and violence on TV is being deliberately introduced from abroad, subsidized."

"To rot America's moral fabric," Blixen said.

"You've read his speech."

"I could have written it."

"Is he loony?" Todd asked.

"Was the senator from Wisconsin?"

"Tell me," Blixen said, "what particular sex and violence is the man referring to, do you know?"

"He claims," Seacliff said, "that he has personally seen female nipples on two network shows, one in prime time—and that his fourteen-year-old son vomited after watching a private detective hit another man in the face with a shovel."

"On which program?" Blixen asked.

Seacliff looked at him. "On *Stagg at Bay,*" he said.

Todd ran the tip of his tongue over his upper front teeth. "Uh-*huh*," he said.

"Now don't jump to conclusions," Seacliff said. "Nobody's going to throw anybody to the wolves. This network has never yet run scared, and it never will."

"I'm glad to hear that, Norman," Blixen said.

"*Stagg* will be renewed or dropped on the basis of demographics, ratings, audience share, growth potential—the same as every other program on our schedule."

"I'm delighted to hear that, Norman," said Blixen.

"I'd just like to ask you one question," Seacliff said. "What in the name of all that's sacred ever prompted you—or your writers—or your director—to have one man hit another man in the face with a shovel?"

"Nothing prompted it," Blixen said. "It was never done."

"Oh, yes, it was—"

"Oh, no, it wasn't. Not on any program of mine."

"You've forgotten . . ."

"No, I haven't."

"Nils, you can't possibly remember every shot on every episode you make."

"I check every shot on every episode I make at least six times, from dailies to answer print! Of course I can remember! Along with everything else, your headline-hunting, half-witted nipple freak is a goddamned liar!"

"Now, now," Todd rumbled.

"He's not *my* nipple freak," Seacliff said.

"That I withdraw," Blixen said. His vision seemed preternaturally sharp—he could make out the broken veins on the side of the green cigar in Todd's mouth—but his own voice sounded miles away to him.

"Who'd like another drink?" he asked. "Sheila?" But when he turned he saw that Sheila had left and that the black maid had reappeared and was threading her way across the living room toward the terrace doors.

"Well, for God's sake," Seacliff said in surprise, "wasn't my wife out here just a minute ago?"

"I thought she was," Todd said.

"Well, that's pretty rude, I must say," Seacliff said.

The maid was waiting.

"Yes, Pauline?" Todd asked.

"Uh—gentleman says his name's Sanderson," Pauline said.

Again Blixen put his glass on the glass-topped table. "I'd better see what he wants."

"Sanderson," Seacliff said. "That's—"

"That's my story editor," Blixen said.

"Oh. Nils, will you take him a message from me?" Seacliff asked. Blixen turned.

"Tell him not to let any more shovels slip by," Seacliff said.

Blixen smiled and Seacliff laughed and gave him the peace sign, but there was no warmth in the gesture, and the eyes were unblinking and very bright over the open, merry mouth. . . .

CHAPTER THREE

"Right down at the end of the hall there, Mr. Blixen," Pauline said, pointing. "Where the little light is."

Blixen nodded and edged his way across the den and past the curved bar where Sheila and Murf Smith were exchanging astrological data and drinking scotch and Frescas.

Astonishingly, he was still so mad that he wasn't certain he could trust his voice. He sat at the narrow telephone table and rested the receiver against his cheek, trying to determine, from what he could remember of Seacliff's words and silences, exactly how critical the situation might be. *Stagg* at best was borderline; it had floundered badly against the big theatrical movies, only surfacing now and again between blockbusters to catch an agonized ratings breath. Still, everyone had assumed that demographics might save it. Its predominately female audience idolized Murphy Smith, and seemed to identify, for some mystic reason, with Isabel. Among women eighteen to thirty-four, it was fourth in popularity—and women eighteen to thirty-four controlled the money, bought the product, counted. But, of course, popularity wasn't the issue. Violence wasn't the issue. Television drama hadn't been allowed to mirror contemporary standards since the 1950s. The issue was an irresponsible politician who ached for eminence, who had the platform and the power to threaten the eunuch TV had become with fresh castrations for old crimes that never had been committed. The question before the House, it seemed to Blixen, was not whether *Stagg* deserved to survive or die—worse shows had survived before this; better ones would die—but whether precensorship by publicity-hungry ward-heelers was to become the order of the day without a single adult voice ever being raised against it.

His heart thudded in his chest. He waited until the band around his temples had loosened a little, then put the receiver to his ear. "Yes, David," he said.

"Hello," Sanderson said. "Nils?"

"Hi—what's happened?"

"Nils," Sanderson said, "uh—I've got a little problem down here and I thought I'd better fill you in on it."

"Down where?" Blixen asked.

"I'm in Oceanport. I'm with Isabel."

"Why? Is Isabel sick?"

"No," Sanderson answered, "not exactly. She's upset, but she's not sick. Did I fill you in about the uncle?"

"The one who has the restaurant?"

"Yes."

"Yes, you did."

"Well—that's where Isabel was today."

"I know. Kapralos told me. He said we had to shoot around her."

"I'm afraid you'll have to shoot around her tomorrow, too, Nils," Sanderson said.

"I don't understand."

"I've already rewritten the scenes. It all works."

"David," Blixen said, "that's really not the point, is it? The point—"

"She says she's not coming in the rest of the week, either," Sanderson said.

Blixen, who was intently bent forward into the alcove over the telephone, sat open-mouthed for a second or two, reading an insurance calendar on the wall in front of his nose.

"Nils?" Sanderson said.

"Oh, she isn't, isn't she," Blixen said.

"That's the little problem I mentioned," Sanderson said. "I reminded her that she had a contract—"

"Is she there?" Blixen asked.

"They're all upstairs, the whole family," Sanderson said. "They're looking for Jesus's gun."

"Jesus's— What for?"

"Well, somebody poisoned his dog tonight," Sanderson explained. "He had this decrepit old poodle and one of these nuts who've been bugging him must have thrown the dog some poisoned meat."

Flatly, Blixen said: "Well, for God's sake."

"Can you believe it?" Sanderson said. "I mean, dirty telephone calls are one thing, poisoning an animal—" He broke off. "Anyway, Jesus thinks he knows who did it—a neighbor named Junkin—hardware dealer—and he claims he's going to kill him."

"Is he serious?"

"I can't tell. I do know he loved that old dog—oh, wait a minute . . . Nils? Isabel's down. I can see her in the kitchen. Do you want to talk to her?"

"Yes."

"Hang on."

Laughter floated through the hallway from Todd's living room; the piano player had shifted to Noel Coward now and someone was singing about lost loves in a dry, innocent voice.

"*Bueno?*" Isabel rasped in Blixen's ear.

"I can always tell when you're going to give me trouble," Blixen said. "You turn Mexican."

"Yeah? Well, that's what I am. Mexican."

"I heard about the dog. I'm shocked and sorry."

"Why? It was just a Mexican's dog."

"Let's start over," Blixen said. "You say *bueno,* and I say *ahijada,* when you're mad and scared, why don't you call me instead of sitting there choking on it? Maybe I could help."

"I'm not scared and nobody's choking," Isabel said, and started to cough. She tried to recover, and couldn't, and was soon gagging and whooping and strangling so badly that she had to hand the phone to Sanderson.

Placatingly Sanderson said: "Can you wait just a second, Nils? One second."

"Of course," Blixen said.

"Here she is."

"If you say something snotty and apt," Isabel grated, "I'll hang up."

"We missed you today," Blixen said.

"Nertz."

"Whatever attractiveness this series possesses comes from the sparks you and Murphy strike together."

"Oh, please."

"Don't you believe it?"

"No."

"It's true."

"All right, it's true," Isabel said. "Who gives a damn?"

"Don't you?"

"As what? A woman? A Mexican, concerned about—"

"As an actress," Blixen said.

Isabel paused. Then, in a lower voice, she said: "Okay, so that strokes my ego a little, yeah. As an actress. But let me tell you something, *patrón*. There are a lot more important flags I fly under than the one marked 'actress.' "

"I'm glad to hear it," Blixen said.

"Like 'Mexican,' for instance."

"Not 'Mexican-American'?"

"That's a cop-out, man. And after three days in this Ramona County paradise, I've decided that I just can't afford any more cop-outs. The Birchers down here don't cop-out, I can promise you. Nobody's a 'Bircher-American.' There's no sentimental crap about constitutional rights or due process or any other of that revolutionary foolishness. These bastards know what they want, and they know how to get it, and it isn't enough anymore for me to sit around wringing my hands and holding Jesus Mary back and waiting for some demented prick to throw a bomb in here and blow my whole family and my friends to smithereens!" She was openly crying now. "Ah, what's the use," she said, "you wouldn't understand."

"Certainly, I—"

"So I'm joining the Army, *patrón*," Isabel said. "I'm going to bomb *them* before they can bomb *me;* I'm going to hate them *harder* than they hate us—and I don't see any way in the world I can do all that and memorize lines, too, do you? My agent'll call you."

"Isabel!"

But she was gone. The phone roared when she dropped it into what sounded like the garbage disposal, but presently the roaring diminished and Sanderson said in shaken accents: "Nils? Are you there?"

"David, what did she mean by that! Where did she go?"

"Jesus found his gun. They've all marched out—"

"What was the roaring? Did he shoot it?"

"The—? Oh! No. I was getting a drink of water and she threw the phone at the hook, but it fell in the sink."

"Do I hear some kind of a thump?"

"That's the aunt—Judith," Sanderson said. "She's alone upstairs now. She wants something. I'd better see . . ."

"Go after Isabel!" Blixen commanded.

"Oh—"

"I'm coming right down."

"Thank God," Sanderson said and hung up.

Blixen listened to the distant buzz of the disconnected phone in his ear for a blank moment, then looked up the number of the nearest cab company, dialed it, and asked for a taxi at Todd's address as soon as possible. He rang his attorney next—a longtime friend named Schreiber—but Schreiber's babysitter said Schreiber was out, so he left his name and got the number of the Ramona County sheriff's office from the information operator and called down there.

"Sheriff's office, Deputy Fry," said the man on the switchboard.

"Hello, my name's Blixen," Blixen said. "I'd like to talk—"

"Address?"

"I beg your pardon?"

"Where are you calling from, Mr. Gibson?" Fry asked.

"Well, I don't necessarily want to report a crime. At least—the crime hasn't happened yet. This is a personal matter. I'm a friend of—"

"Mr. Gibson?"

"Yes."

"Where are you calling from, sir?"

"Los Angeles," Blixen said.

"You've dialed the Ramona County sheriff's office," Fry said. "If you live in unincorporated territory, please call the L.A. sheriff. If you're in the city, call the L.A. police. Do you have those numbers?"

"I can look them up," Blixen said.

"Thank you," Fry said. "Good night."

"Good night," Blixen said. He sat for a moment rubbing his fingertips gently over his right eyebrow, and then he depressed the receiver bar and redialed.

"Sheriff's office, Deputy Fry," Fry said.

"I'm afraid I have a bad cold," Blixen said hoarsely. "Can you hear me?"

"Yes, I can."

"My name is Robert E. Smith," Blixen said, "and I'm calling from one-one-four and a half Pelham Avenue, Ramona City. I'm on the committee to re-elect Sheriff DeGroot. Is he there? I'd like to get some information from him."

"One-one-four—"

"And a half."

"And a half," Fry said. "Just a minute."

There were a number of clicks and then DeGroot said cautiously: "Who is this again?"

"Nils-Frederik Blixen," Blixen said. "How are you, Teet?"

"Well, for crying out loud," DeGroot said, "Nils!"

"Teet, who's the law in Oceanport now? Do they have a local police force, or—"

"I'm the law," DeGroot said. "They use county police, county fire . . . Nils, excuse me." The phone was lowered, and covered, while DeGroot gave someone a number of orders in a querulous undertone, and then a door slammed and DeGroot said: "Now—what was all this about Robert E. Smith? We were having you traced, taped for a voice print."

"You were? Why?"

"Robert E. Smith? One-one-four and a half—"

"That doesn't sound so crazy to me."

"Fry said you'd called in a minute before, though."

"Oh, he recognized my voice."

"He said you gave the name Gibson and then called back and pretended you had a cold and told him you were Robert E. Smith. We thought we had the King of the Butterflies in the net there for a minute. Why 'Gibson'?"

"Not 'Gibson.' 'Blixen.'"

"Bl—ah. Ah."

"We just didn't seem to be communicating," Blixen said, "so I—" He stopped. "Well, it doesn't matter. I'm sorry I shook everybody up."

"We'll recover."

"Teet, let me tell you why I called," Blixen said. "Have you seen my series?"

"Love it."

"The girl who plays Raquel, the secretary, has an uncle in Oceanport, a man named Jesus Chavez. He runs a Mexican restaurant there."

"In *Oceanport?*" DeGroot said, awed.

"Anyway, there's been a good deal of trouble lately. Obscene phone calls, broken windows—"

"We never heard anything about that."

"Uncle Jesus doesn't believe in the police," Blixen said.

"Got you."

"Then tonight," Blixen said, "someone poisoned his dog."

After a moment DeGroot said: "Where did you say Uncle Jesus was located again?"

"I don't know his address."

"Well, Oceanport can't have but the one Mexican restaurant."

"He's also armed and I'm afraid he thinks he knows who did the poisoning," Blixen said.

"And would you have that person's name?" DeGroot asked. "The suspected poisoner?"

"Junkin."

"We'll look into it right away."

"Thank you, Teet."

"Girl with her uncle at the moment?"

"Yes, she is."

"Don't worry. There won't be any reporters."

After DeGroot hung up, Blixen attempted to reach Schreiber once more, but before he had finished dialing, the maid, Pauline, materialized at his elbow. "Mr. Blixen?" she whispered. "Did you order a cab?"

"Yes! Is he here?"

"He's turning around—"

"Is Mr. Todd still on the terrace?"

"No, sir," Pauline said, and nodded back toward the den, where Todd was eating peanuts out of a shallow silver bowl and waiting like a spider for him.

Blixen replaced the receiver. "I had a coat, Pauline."

"Yes, sir, gray one, I'll get it."

Todd met him halfway down the hall. "About ready to rejoin the party, are you, boy?" he asked in a silken voice. "I don't want to remind you of your manners, but telephone calls are for the office. We're here to court our old friend Norm, dull as that may be."

"I'm afraid you'll have to court him alone from now on, Art," Blixen said.

Todd lifted an eyebrow.

"My star's in trouble," Blixen said.

"What's he into this time," Todd asked. "Drugs?"

"Not that star," Blixen said. "Isabel."

"Send somebody else. Is she in jail? What's she done?"

"Nothing. She's emotionally upset."

Todd, who was looking around for something solid to put the silver bowl on, stopped so short that several peanuts fell to the floor.

"I'll fill you in tomorrow, Arthur," Blixen said. Pauline approached with his coat, and he held his hand out to take it. "She's worried about her uncle. They've—"

"I see your lips moving," Todd said, "but the words don't make any sense. Maybe I've had a stroke."

"Right," Blixen said. "Well—"

"Or if I haven't, I will. Are you seriously threatening to walk out of a party as important as this just to hold that pop-eyed Chicana's hand for an hour or two?"

"That's what I'm seriously threatening, yes," Blixen said. "I'll see you tomorrow."

"Wait a minute!" Todd snapped. He crunched over the spilled peanuts and stood glaring up into Blixen's eyes. "Are you sure you're in the right business? Diplomacy runs this trade, boy—friendships, one hand washing the other. I've seen bigger programs than yours wind up on the trash heap because somebody thought somebody else insulted him. Now, you spoke your piece loud and clear to our friend out on the terrace there, and he didn't appreciate it one bit. He misunderstood you all the way around. He thought you blamed him for not standing up enough to Connaught—"

"Then he didn't misunderstand after all."

"He misunderstood," Todd repeated stubbornly. "I told him I remembered the shovel scene, and that I also remembered you saying how you planned to cut it, but that it must have slipped by you somehow."

"Arthur, you really amaze me sometimes."

"I told him we'd cut it out now, however, and that he could assure Connaught it would never be in the rerun."

"I'll bet that eased his mind."

"The point is that it may save your series. It's called *diplomacy*."

"It's called bullshit," Blixen said.

"You be careful," Todd said. "Just about one more good pull on the saw and you're going to cut right through that limb you're sitting on."

"No doubt," Blixen said. "Well . . ."

"You know, boy," Todd said, "the studio can sure get along without *Stagg,* but can NFB Productions get along without the studio *or* the network?"

"Good question," Blixen said. He waved. "Say good night to Sheila for me."

"Nils!"

Again Blixen glanced around.

Todd's face was beet-red. "I told him I'd bring you upstairs for a drink. Just the three of us. He's waiting. What do I tell him now?"

Blixen frowned at the floor, thinking. "Well, Jesus, Arthur," he said, "I don't know. . . . Why don't you just say I had some wood to saw?"

He smiled again and waved again, and again set off down the paneled hall, shrugging into his warm gray coat as he went.

CHAPTER FOUR

Oceanport, unplanned and wooden, hung on the hills above the sea like a Kansas town tipped sideways. Nothing in it spoke of California; the main east and west streets were Sunflower and Leavenworth and Capper and Kaw, the north and south ran a reduced gamut from A to M.

They stopped at an Arco station on E to get their bearings, and the blond attendant in the army jacket and the cords told Blixen that he didn't know of any Mexican restaurants around there, but that if there was one, it was probably on A, near the water. He instructed the cab driver to proceed straight down Sunflower to the old highway, which was A, and then bear south. He was the politest boy Blixen had ever met, with the exception of Pat Boone. There were two old, luminous red, white, and blue bumper stickers on the station's tow truck: RE-ELECT RICHARD M. NIXON and GOD SAVE AMERICA.

"I don't know the name of this cafe," Blixen said to the driver when they turned on A, "but it ought to be near a hardware store called Junkin's."

"Uh-oh," said the driver.

"Now what?"

"Cops," the driver said. "Looks like a safety inspection. Well, I can swing—"

"No, it's all right," Blixen said. "Pull up to the barricade. There's the restaurant."

It was a square, blistered building, blazing with lights, two stories high, marred by an ornate midwestern cornice and a buckling wooden staircase pasted against its northern wall. Every window on the street side of the second floor had been broken, and GO HOME BASTARD COMMIE had been spray-painted in red on the downstairs door. No one had been able to break the large, half-frosted front window, although a number of contestants had tried. Lines radiated through the gold of CHAVEZ' LA CUCARACHA—AUTHENTIC MEXICAN CUISINE like the slender cracks on a barely iced pond. A man pacing in front of the cracked window stopped when he saw the cab, and then began running toward it, leaping over the rain-filled potholes. Sanderson.

"What those people need is a few more lights," the cab driver said. "What are they holding down there, a wake?"

He nosed to a stop against the police barricade on the ocean side of the street. Beyond the narrow, pancake-colored beach, the Pacific curled and broke deafeningly. The air, sharp as a razor, smelled of rotting fish and seaweed. Sanderson, a step ahead of the barricade guard, shaded his eyes and peered mistrustfully through the back window at Blixen, who gestured a greeting and then handed the driver a five and a ten and said: "That's fine, thanks."

Opening the rear door, Sanderson said: "You made it." He was wearing a porkpie hat, a Scottish raincoat, and the first pair of rubbers Blixen had seen on adult male feet in forty years. The strain he was under had darkened his eyes, rounded his shoulders. "Come on, they're waiting."

"How's Isabel?"

"Don't ask."

But the barricade guard had one question for Blixen before they could proceed. "Mr. Junkin?" he inquired, smiling.

"I'm sorry, no, my name's Blixen."

"I see," the guard said.

"This is Miss Chavez's boss," Sanderson said.

"Check," said the guard. He was a crew-cut young deputy, as healthy and polite as an FBI man. He returned to the barricade and motioned the cab on, then stood with his hands clasped behind his back, beaming at Blixen.

"This way," Sanderson said. "Be careful of the potholes. They haven't fixed this street since it was built."

"Tell me something," Blixen muttered. "Why do I feel so convinced I'm about to be shot in the back?"

"Isn't that wild?" Sanderson said. "Any minute. Phhhht. I think it's because they grin all the time."

"How does Uncle Jesus react to these boys?"

"Three guesses."

"Well, at least he hasn't killed anyone. Or can I presume that?"

"Oh, I hope so," Sanderson said. "He couldn't find Junkin. Or he claims he couldn't."

"Claims?"

"Well, here's what happened. They all tore out of here around—when did I call you?"

"About ten."

"About ten, blood in their eyes, but Junkin wasn't home. He's got a place over on Capper. Anyway, by the time I got there, Isabel and Mrs. Junkin were screaming at each other and Mrs. Billroth was trying to calm the two of them down."

"Who's Mrs. Billroth?"

"A friend of the family. She looks after the sick aunt."

"What about Jesus?"

"Jesus was gone. Jesus was back *here,*" Sanderson said. They'd reached the sidewalk in front of the garishly lighted restaurant and Sanderson now pointed toward the squat building abutting La Cucaracha on the north. "That's Junkin's store," he said.

"Ah."

"Well, for some crazy reason, Jesus decided that Junkin was hiding out in there, so he broke in."

Blixen stared. "He—"

"I know, I know, I know," Sanderson said. "Wait, though, I haven't gotten to the *good* part yet. He was in there, alone, for about twenty minutes before the police came."

"Burglar alarm?"

"No, apparently these were the police *you* called, the sheriff himself."

"DeGroot," Blixen said.

"DeGroot, correct."

"He's here, then."

"*Boy,* is he here," Sanderson said, and shook his hand as though it had just been pinched in a terrible trap.

"Oh, Teet's all right," Blixen said irritably. "I've known Teet for years, we grew up together in Portland."

"'Teet'?"

"It was Lester to begin with, but his little brother couldn't say that," Blixen explained, "so he got to be Teeter and then finally it was just Teet."

"Well, don't tell Isabel, I beg of you," Sanderson said. "That's about the only thing she hasn't called him yet."

Angrily Blixen said: "David, I don't understand this. The man's down here to help. What's he done that's so unforgivable?"

"Well," Sanderson said, "how about accusing Jesus of murder, for openers?"

Inside the restaurant, something crashed and a woman began to curse in Spanish. The wind had grown icier. Blixen raised his coat collar and held it closed against his throat. "Murder," he repeated pensively.

But Sanderson had cocked his head to listen to the Spanish oaths and shrieks. "Can that be Gloria?" he asked in wonder.

"Who's Gloria?"

"The quiet one," Sanderson said. "Jesus's girl."

"David," Blixen said, "I know you think you've given me this whole remarkable story in the most clear, concise—"

"What puzzles you?"

"Who," Blixen asked, "is Jesus supposed to have murdered?"

"Why, Junkin," Sanderson said, "naturally."

"But if Junkin hasn't been located, if there's no evidence of—"

"Did I tell you that there was one bullet gone from Jesus's gun?"

"No, you didn't."

"He claims he shot at a rat Saturday and forgot to clean the chamber."

"And DeGroot doesn't believe that?"

"DeGroot," Sanderson said, "asked to see the rat. Jesus said he'd missed. DeGroot asked to see the bullet hole. Jesus told him to take a flying fling at the moon. I think he said 'fling.' "

"But Jesus is right! There's no reason for Teet to assume—"

"Well," Sanderson began, then glowered at the sidewalk and stopped.

Blixen thrust his head forward a little. "Well, what?"

"Well, it seems," Sanderson continued reluctantly, "that there may just be one other slight hitch. DeGroot began checking around, and no one's seen Junkin since Saturday. He told his wife that Jesus had threatened him—and then he just disappeared."

The Spanish cursing had stopped now. Sanderson took a deep breath and put his hand on the Cucaracha's red-smeared doorknob. "So," he said. "Are you ready?"

CHAPTER FIVE

Blixen's first impression of Jesus Mary's restaurant was of grass, marijuana, the curling, sweet smell of Acapulco gold in the smoke-stained air. DeGroot, a bull of a man, sat at a table for two against the wall, his head thrown back and a wet cloth pressed to his bloody nose. He was out of uniform, dressed in a brown suit and a snowy, gore-spotted sport shirt. When he felt the cold wind from the open front door on his ankles, he turned his entire upper body and feebly waved his free hand.

"My God, what have they done to him?" Blixen muttered.

"I'm afraid to think," Sanderson muttered back.

"Is that Jesus? On the phone?"

Sanderson followed his gaze. "Yes."

Isabel, who had been gesticulating in the kitchen doorway at a round-faced, frightened young man in a yellow slicker and a coonskin cap, spotted them now, and marched past DeGroot and up to Sanderson. "You will never *believe* what just happened!" she howled.

"We heard the crash—"

"*This* officious clown," Isabel ranted on, pointing at DeGroot, "decides out of a clear blue sky to search the place for pot. No warrant, no may-I, no nothing. If you're Mexican, you're on the stuff, right? So here he goes—under the counter, into the sugar bowls, comes to the kitchen"—she twisted around to jab her thumb toward the swinging door—"charges straight through—knocks Gloria right on her tokus—"

"That *was* Gloria," Sanderson said. "I didn't realize she knew so many dirty words."

"Neither did Gloria. She was carrying that beautiful old clay dish of Mama's from Pueblo? Gone! Busted into a thousand pieces. Cabral's in there now trying to calm her down. *Pobrecita.*"

"But it was DeGroot who got the bloody nose," Blixen pointed out.

"Brouwer and Dr. Trout both came by," Isabel went on to Sanderson, as though Blixen weren't standing there. "Did you see 'em?"

"Is Brouwer the boy in the coonskin cap?"

"Yeah, the minister." She stretched, trying to peer into the kitchen. "I guess Trout's upstairs with Judy. . . ."

"Isabel," Blixen began.

"You can imagine what all this hysteria has done to her back."

"Isabel, don't be childish," Blixen said, "look at me." And then he did something that he'd known from the instinctive beginning he shouldn't, though perhaps it was the only course that could ever have worked, the one distasteful cue the actress inside her was waiting for. He took her upper arm to turn her about, and she sprang at him like a freed coil and whacked him squarely across the cheek. He couldn't recall ever being hit harder; he fell back in dismay and pain, scarcely aware of what she was yelling: ". . . *knew* how we felt—you *knew* how those rotten *cops* would treat us, but you *called* them!"

"Isabel—"

But she had already broken free, crying and lurching into every stool along the counter on her blind way out.

Little by little Blixen realized that he was the center of a remarkable tableau. On his left, Jesus Mary stood with the phone clamped to his ear, jaw hanging. DeGroot, to his right, squinted at him like a gaudy parrot over his swollen beak. Three astonished figures hovered in the open kitchen doorway: the boy in the coonskin cap, a curly-haired older man, and a red-eyed bovine girl whom Blixen took to be Gloria. It was Jesus Mary who first found his tongue. Incredulously he told the telephone he'd call it back, and then he savagely surged out after his niece. Behind Blixen, Sanderson kept groaning: "Oh, my God . . . oh, my God . . ."

"David," Blixen got out through his numb lips, "is there a chair back there anywhere you could push over in this direction?"

"She's not herself tonight, Nils," Sanderson moaned. "She's distraught."

"You know, I sensed that?" Blixen said.

Twice Sanderson made the round trip between the door and Blixen before opting for fence-mending over love. "Here—my God . . ."

The edge of a metal chair brushed Blixen's calves and he allowed Sanderson to help him into it. The left side of his face had begun to glow and itch from temple to jaw; he palpated it, half afraid to check his fingertips afterward. But there was no blood.

"How do you feel?" Sanderson asked. "She packs a terrible wallop, doesn't she?"

"I hope you never have to know how terrible."

"I do know. She hit me once back in September."

"You're kidding."

"Loosened a tooth," Sanderson insisted. He opened his mouth and bent down to waggle the tooth in question with his forefinger. "It symbolizes something to her," he said thickly.

"That loose tooth?" Blixen asked.

"No, hitting, hitting," Sanderson said.

"Anger, perhaps."

"All right, mock," Sanderson snapped. "I know what I mean."

Blixen fetched a breath from out of the depths of his chest. "Yes. So do I."

Sullenly Sanderson waited.

"You mean," Blixen went on, "that it's more than emotional. More than spur-of-the-moment. More—planned than that. . . ." He paused to reflect. "It's almost as if she wanted retaliation of some kind."

"Well, I wouldn't go so far—"

"What do you think she wanted from you?" Blixen asked. "In September?"

After a while, Sanderson said: "I think she wanted me to split, disappear."

"And from me just now?"

Sanderson opened his mouth and then closed it again. In the background, the three figures had vanished. "Listen, Nils, I'll tell you what she *doesn't* want," Sanderson said tensely, "she doesn't want you to fire her, don't get that into your head!"

"She told me tonight she was quitting."

"She didn't mean it."

"Oh, I think she did."

Excited, Sanderson cried: "Baloney. I can't imagine anything easier—or dumber—than to take somebody up on a threat made in—in—made in—"

"Neither can I," Blixen said. "Nor more destructive."

"What do you want to do, wreck the series? She *is* the series!"

"I know that," Blixen said. "I won't let her quit."

"And in the third place," Sanderson shouted, "what makes you so bloody sure I wouldn't go with her?"

"I think you would," Blixen said.

"Oh, yes, I would," Sanderson shouted, "and you know I would!" He pried a pipe out of his raincoat pocket and thrust it between his teeth, walking raggedly around and breathing shallowly and loudly. "Make no mistake about that, buddy," he said. He snatched the pipe out of his mouth and rubbed the bowl against his nose, checking the grain of the wood. "What did you say?" he asked.

"Nothing," Blixen said. "When?"

"Back there a ways."

"I said I wouldn't let her quit," Blixen repeated. "She's too important to me. I love her too much."

Sanderson chewed on his pipe for a time and then raised his chin and massaged his throat. "Nils, did you ever have the kind of a day," he asked, "when you just wanted to lie down and kick and scream and wet in the mud?"

"I'm in the middle of one now," Blixen said.

"But you never let yourself go."

"I did tonight," Blixen said. "At Todd's party."

Sanderson was able to smile, eyes closed. "I wish I'd seen that. What happened?"

"If we're canceled, I'll tell you."

The eyes opened. "Are we being canceled?"

"Who knows?" Blixen said. "Let's you and Isabel and me just get through this season."

"Let's do that," Sanderson murmured. He rebuttoned his raincoat, gazing toward the door and the black street. "I guess I'd better go find her. She gets these migraines—never looks where she's headed . . . She was almost run over the first night she got here."

"Run—! What happened?"

"Nothing. I mean, it scared her, but she wasn't hurt. She took a walk after dinner and tried to cross some street against the signal. The car came close enough to rip the coat she was wearing."

"Good God! Did he stop?"

"Going too fast," Sanderson said. Uneasily he removed his porkpie hat and slapped it against his leg. "Well," he added, "Nils—I—"

"It's forgotten," Blixen said.

"What is?"

"Weren't you intending to apologize?"

"Not now, you're too sure of yourself," Sanderson said.

Blixen grinned and Sanderson smiled shyly back, stuck the pipe in his mouth upside down, and tramped out into the chilly night to find his woman.

CHAPTER SIX

"Alone at last," DeGroot said.

Blixen swiveled his head and DeGroot took away the cloth from his nose and refolded it until he'd found a corner that was still white, then pressed that against his upper lip. The bleeding had stopped by now, although DeGroot appeared unable to believe it and continued to toy with his injury. "I think," he said, "that this has been the most bizarre hour and a half I've ever lived through."

"Is that a fact," Blixen said.

"Absolutely bizarre," DeGroot said.

"Teet," Blixen said, "I want to ask you a serious question."

"The answer is yes," DeGroot replied. "She saw me coming through the little window—she timed it—and she pushed when the time was ripe. She wanted to break my nose. I'll go to my grave believing that."

"I see," Blixen said. "Well, that wasn't exactly the question I had in mind, but I suppose it'll get us started."

"All police officers are pigs to these people," DeGroot said.

"Did *you* see the girl?"

"When?"

"Through the little window."

"I was thinking about something more important."

"Like who poisoned the dog?" Blixen suggested.

DeGroot rubbed the back of a finger over the mustache of dried blood on his upper lip, eyeing Blixen contemplatively.

"Well?" Blixen asked.

"No," DeGroot said, "like where had they hidden the hash." His Dutch eyes were wet and still under the tangled blond brows. "Don't goad me, Nils," he added. "No more games. For two cents I'd jail this whole spic crew."

"Possession of marijuana?"

"When I find it."

"Who do you jail when you find it in the Ramona City Country Club, Teet?"

"I told you, don't goad me."

"Or one of your own sheriff's department men's rooms?"

"No spics on my force," DeGroot said. He dropped the cloth on the table, rested his straw-colored head against the wall, and placed his hands flat on his knees. The hands moved with a life of their own, kneading softly. "You don't understand this situation," he said.

"Oh, I think I do."

"No, you don't. This Chavez has a record as long as your arm. Did you know he was a Communist?"

"No."

"He is. Brags about it. Your star's uncle is an avowed member of the Communist conspiracy."

"They don't seem to go together, do they?"

"What doesn't?"

" 'Avowed' and 'conspiracy.' I had the impression that conspiracies were usually kept secret. Like Watergate."

But DeGroot wasn't listening. "You want more, I'll give you more. Suspicion of robbery. Suspicion of bookmaking—"

"Any convictions?"

"Then you've got your civil suits," DeGroot went on, "paternity charge in Bliss, Texas, any number of—"

"Regular one-man gang."

"They're animals, these people."

"Teet," Blixen said, "do you remember Phyllis Tanaka?"

The big hands quieted.

"Well, maybe that was too long ago," Blixen said.

"What do you want me to say? Yes, I remember Phyllis Tanaka. All right?"

"They were animals, those people," Blixen said.

"Keep it up, keep it up," DeGroot said. A muscle began to flinch in his cheek. He raised a finger, ostensibly to test the reddish crust under his nose, really to hide the flinch. "We were kids, there's no parallel, that was a very emotional time. . . ."

December 8, 1941, a numb Monday. No one had known what to do, so the schools were open, more or less. Phyllis Tanaka, born on July 4, 1929, to nisei parents in Portland, Oregon, thought of herself as American, until fifteen minutes of nine, when seven boys her own age caught her crossing Fremont Street toward the school grounds and beat her nearly to death. None of the boys was ever prosecuted, nor even caught, although the police made several discreet inquiries. The only serious clamor raised in her behalf came from a neighbor none of the parents liked much, a rough kid named Lester De-Groot. DeGroot kept asking what the shit was going on when little girls could be openly attacked without anybody caring?

His friends (including Nils-Frederik Blixen) ardently assured him that people cared—Americans always cared—but that there was now a war on, and that innocents always got hurt in a war. What about the little American girls at Pearl Harbor, they challenged, who had been ripped to pieces by Nip bombs?

What about the American girl on Fremont Street, DeGroot hollered back, who had been kicked in the head by *American feet?*

She was *Japanese,* they kept screaming at him, *Japanese,* look at her goddamn *eyes!* They're all alike, those people, they're treacherous, they never give up, they're *animals,* those people. . . .

"I wonder what ever happened to Phyllis," DeGroot murmured.

"I understand Phyllis stayed on in St. Paul," Blixen said.

"Is that where they relocated the family?"

"Somewhere in that area. St. Paul, Minneapolis . . ."

"Long time ago," DeGroot said.

"Odd how the enemies change."

DeGroot's eyes sought the smoky ceiling. "Mine never have."

"You still don't see a parallel between Phyllis and these people?"

"I see the parallel you'd like to make."

"But you don't see Chavez as a victim, even after the broken windows and the paint on the door."

"Bear comes up the pike, spots a honey hive," DeGroot said, "breaks in, the bees sting him. Who's the victim?"

"We're talking about human beings, not bears and bees."

"We're talking about a Communist whose whole philosophy is to redistribute the honey the Americans in this county have sweated their guts out all their lives to make and save. So they stung him. It's in the nature of bees to sting."

"And bears to steal."

"Yes, and bears to steal."

"What was it this particular bear stole, Teet?"

"This particular bear," DeGroot began, and stopped. "It's what Communists represent that counts, my friend, and you know it as well as I do—what they intend."

"So these particular bees sought out this particular bear in his own cave and stung him on general principles, out of panic."

"They had a right to panic," DeGroot said.

"As much right as the kids in Portland who kicked Phyllis in the head before she could sabotage the Kaiser shipyards?"

"Keep it up," DeGroot said, "keep it up." But his eyes had grown puzzled and darker; the flinch had slowed.

"Let's talk about the Portland cops," Blixen said. "You told me a thousand times they could have found those kids if they'd tried. Were they right to let the case drop?"

"There was a war on."

"Were they right or wrong?"

"I'm not about to judge men who might have had—"

"Were they right or wrong?"

"Jesus *Christ!*" DeGroot bellowed. "Will you get off my back!" What do you want from me? All right, they were wrong! I don't need you to teach me Sunday school scripture! You're not my conscience, okay? Okay?"

"Okay," Blixen said.

"*Big* deal," DeGroot said, and gave a sardonic laugh which started his nose bleeding again. "Oh, hell," he said in exhaustion.

"Lean your head back," Blixen told him.

"It's still—"

"I'll get another cloth."

"No, hit the ceiling!"

"The what?"

"Hit the ceiling, the ceiling!" DeGroot waved wildly toward a broom in the corner and bawled: "Doctor?"

Blixen grabbed the broom, hoisted it, and hit the ceiling.

CHAPTER SEVEN

He tumbled down the back stairs and came loping in from the kitchen sixty seconds later like a boy on an imaginary horse. "What did you do, pick it?" he cried accusingly. He had a long, brown, old face and the sweet, sad eyes of a bloodhound. He peered, through the bottoms of bifocal glasses, up DeGroot's nose and touched the bridge with feather-soft arthritic fingers. "When did this start?"

"Just now," Blixen said. "He got a little excited."

"You didn't strike him?"

"What? No! Strike him? No."

"I meant accidentally."

"No, no."

"Well, it's not broken. I told him that. But if it doesn't stop in ten or fifteen minutes, we'd better take him to the hospital."

"It'll stop," DeGroot promised grimly.

"Trout," the old man said to Blixen.

"Oh," DeGroot said, "Dr. Trout, Nils Blixen, Mr. Blixen, Dr. Trout."

"You make *Stagg at Bay!*" Dr. Trout exclaimed jubilantly.

"Yes! Have you seen it?"

"No, I haven't," Trout replied. "But then I see so little television. I'm not really a TV fan."

"Well, you're not alone," Blixen said.

"I remember one program, though," Trout said, "about a surgeon who began to develop a conflict over blood, couldn't bear the sight of blood. Do you know why?"

"Haven't a clue," Blixen said.

"This came out after his death," Trout said. "He kept sitting up on the autopsy table. He'd been a famous surgeon by day but a vampire by night. I laughed until I cried. I knew how they all felt. I was once one myself." He looked startled. "A coroner, coroner! Not a vampire."

"How did they solve the problem?" Blixen asked.

"Oh, the only way they could," Trout said. "They drove a stake through his heart." DeGroot chuckled and Trout examined the battered nose again through his bifocals. "Well, I think that's all right now," he said. "Stand up."

Cautiously DeGroot pushed back his chair and straightened to his full height. His eyes glittered anxiously.

"How does that feel?" Trout asked.

"Pretty good."

"Just don't blow it."

"No."

"Where's Jesus?" The old doctor sat in DeGroot's chair to scrawl a prescription on a dog-eared pad with a thick gold pen. He had unbuttoned his black coat to fish the pad out of his vest pocket; a golden watch chain hung across his stomach. His starched shirt cuffs, Blixen noticed, were badly frayed. There was a hole in the bottom of one high-top shoe. "Tell him this is a sedative for his wife. He ought to pick it up tonight."

"How's she feeling?" DeGroot asked.

"Still in pain. It's mostly emotional, and of course the death of the dog hasn't helped."

"Can I question her?"

Trout slumped back in the chair, puzzled, capping his big pen. "What on earth for? She wasn't down here when the dog died. She couldn't possibly—"

"Not about the dog," DeGroot said. "I want to know when she saw Junkin last."

Warningly Blixen murmured: "Teet . . ."

"Goddamn it," DeGroot said through clenched teeth, "when I decide to abdicate the responsibilities of this office and sit around weeping into my vodka with the rest of you pinko bleeding hearts, I'll tell you, Nils, fair enough? In the meantime—with your permission—I'd like to get on with the case in hand."

"The great marijuana caper . . ."

"Screw the marijuana. Any unsmoked pot around here was flushed down the toilet ten seconds after I walked in."

"Oh, is *that* what that smell is?" Trout inquired. "Roofers?"

"Reefers, reefers," DeGroot snapped.

"And just what *is* the case in hand, Sheriff?" Blixen asked.

"The disappearance of George Junkin!"

"Not the attacks on Jesus Mary Chavez?"

"I think they're linked!"

"Based on what?"

"On certain statements made by—" DeGroot stopped short, evidently aware for the first time of the volume of his own voice. He pulled up another chair, sat down, and stretched his neck against the imaginary restriction of a nonexistent collar. "All right, I telephoned the Junkin residence," he said in a lower, tighter tone, "five minutes after you called me. I wanted to alert them to the fact that Chavez was armed and on the warpath. But Mrs. Junkin said she hadn't seen her husband since Saturday. She said she was worried sick, that she'd called every relative and friend she could think of, and that she'd been about to notify the police. I asked her if Junkin had ever disappeared like this before—on a bender, for instance— and she said no, he never had."

"George is a patient of mine," Trout said. "I don't believe he's ever touched a drop of liquor in his life. Might have helped him if he had."

"Anyway," DeGroot said, "it seems he went to work at the usual time on Saturday—he opened the store around ten—and then he telephoned her at three-thirty to tell her not to fix dinner for him. He said he'd made an appointment with a lawyer named Hopkins in San Diego, and that he'd eat with Hopkins and be home around midnight. Mrs. Junkin said that was fine because her mother wasn't feeling well and she'd half promised to spend the night over there anyway. Junkin told her to do that by all means, and hung up."

"And dropped out of sight," Blixen said, "like a stone down a well."

"Nils, if you think this is funny, I'm sorry for you," DeGroot said.

"I don't think it's funny at all, Sheriff. I think it's classic." Blixen glanced at Trout. "Doctor—what did you mean when you said a little liquor might have helped Junkin?"

"*Well,*" Trout said and pursed his lips.

"How old a man are we talking about here?"

"Oh—fifty, fifty-one . . ."

"Conservative? Church-going? Tee-totaler?"

"Yes."

"Nils," DeGroot began.

"Just a minute. If I'm embarrassing the doctor, he'll tell me. I'm not asking him to reveal any medical secrets."

"No, I know what you're asking me," Trout admitted, "and, do you know, I believe you may be right." He tapped the corner of the prescription pad on the table, brow furrowed. "Classic. Yes . . . I *told* him the only way he'd get rid of his backache was to unbend."

"What backache?" DeGroot exploded. "What the hell are you talking about?"

"Unbending," Blixen said. "Waking up one morning at fifty to the same drab work, the same drab wife . . ."

"How do you know she's drab?" DeGroot demanded.

"Oh, she's drab," Trout murmured.

"I know it can't be much of a marriage," Blixen said, "when the husband disappears on a Saturday and the wife hasn't yet gotten around to reporting it to the police by the following Monday."

"She called all their friends."

"Did she call the lawyer, Hopkins?"

"She did," DeGroot said. "And so did I."

"With what result?"

"Junkin never showed up for his late-afternoon appointment."

"I don't suppose either one of you asked what the meeting was to have been about?"

"Well, as it happens," DeGroot said, "I did, yeah."

"Women?" Dr. Trout asked. "Some . . . entanglement with—"

"Threats," DeGroot said. "Mr. Junkin wanted a rundown on the slander laws. As Hopkins understood it, a neighbor named Chavez had been publicly accusing Junkin of mental and physical harassment, and had even threatened to kill Junkin if he didn't stop. Junkin wanted to know what legal steps he could take to protect himself and his wife from this Mexican maniac."

"My word," Dr. Trout said, and glanced at Blixen.

"So," Blixen said slowly, "you immediately assumed—"

"I assume nothing, I just want to know two things," DeGroot said. "First, who did Jesus Chavez shoot at Saturday—and what was he doing for twenty minutes alone in Junkin's store tonight?"

"He told you what he was doing."

"He told me he was looking for Junkin! Which doesn't make any more sense than—"

"All right, what's *your* explanation?"

"I think there was a fight Saturday," DeGroot said. "I think Chavez shot Junkin some time after three-thirty, and I think he was over there tonight making mighty sure he hadn't forgotten some sweet little clue that could send him to the gas chamber."

"Teet," Blixen began, and then stopped, shaking his head.

"And if that's what *did* happen," DeGroot said, "I'm going to prove it if I have to lock every technician on my staff into that hardware store for the next ten years. There'll be something. Blood in a linoleum crack. Hair on a—"

"Sheriff?" Blixen said. "How many technicians are you going to lock onto the dog-poisoning case?"

"You know what wouldn't surprise me?" DeGroot said. "If that commie Aztec didn't poison the dog himself—to keep us off balance about Junkin—to . . ."

Blixen's expressionless eyes held his steadily.

DeGroot's ears reddened and the flinch returned. "Well, don't goad me," he muttered.

"Doctor," Blixen said.

Trout jumped. "Yes."

"Have you seen the dog?"

"Yes. They have it in a box on the back porch."

"Do you have any idea what sort of poison was used?"

"Oh, strychnine, I'd say. There were all the earmarks. Opisthotonos—"

"What's opisthotonos?"

"It's an arching of the back," Trout said, "a spasm of the back, neck, and legs—very typical. Jesus told me the dog spasmed repeatedly while he was holding it. Not a pretty sight."

"What had the dog eaten?"

"Nobody knows. Jesus was outside, in front, when his daughter ran up screaming that something was wrong with Harpo. He found the dog in the kitchen, thrashing around under the stove. He pulled it out and it died in his lap."

DeGroot raised his head. "Are you saying it was poisoned in the kitchen then? That it found something there—under the stove?"

"They just aren't sure."

"Well, but—"

"Strychnine doesn't work that fast," Trout explained. "Takes, oh, ten, fifteen minutes before the symptoms set in. And Harpo had the run of the house, so he could have picked it up almost anywhere."

"In the yard?" Blixen asked.

"Oh, yes indeed," Trout replied. "There's a dog door."

"So someone could have thrown a piece of meat over the fence?"

"Yes."

"And Harpo might have gulped it down, returned to the kitchen—"

"Yes, yes."

Outside, a car door slammed; heels clacked across the sidewalk. Isabel, hands framing her face, glared through the cracked front window. When she caught Blixen's eyes on hers, she stiffened and spun away.

"Doctor," Blixen resumed, "who might normally have access to strychnine?"

"Well, I might, for one," Trout said. "It's used medically."

"I think exterminators use it, too."

"On rats," Trout said, nodding. "All kinds of vermin, yes."

"Next question," DeGroot said in a mocking drawl. "Do hardware dealers ever stock commercial vermin-exterminators?"

Wide-eyed, Blixen glanced up.

DeGroot laughed and rubbed his big hands over his face.

"Naturally, though, you'll check it out, Sheriff," Blixen said.

"Oh, naturally, naturally," DeGroot said.

"When's the P.M.?"

"What P.M.?"

"On the dog."

DeGroot continued to rub his face for a while, then lowered his hands and rested his chin on his steepled fingers. "You know, Nils, I'm really getting sick and tired of this," he said.

"You know, Teet," Blixen said, "so am I."

"You want an official inquest into the death of that dog now?"

"No, I want an official autopsy."

"You'll get it."

"When?"

"I don't know when," DeGroot said. "When there's time. When the important parts of this case begin to gel. There's no mystery about the dog. We know how the dog died. The dog was poisoned. That's regrettable. My heart aches for the people who loved him. But there are also people who loved George Junkin."

"George Junkin could turn up tomorrow."

"If George Junkin turns up tomorrow," DeGroot said, "alive, and if he's had any access at all to strychnine, we'll hold him for questioning. Does that satisfy you?"

"No," Blixen said.

"Tough," DeGroot said.

"In the first place," Blixen said, "there *is* no George Junkin case, so don't try to bargain with bait that doesn't exist. In the second place, how do you know the strychnine was meant for the dog?"

Dr. Trout, probing an itch in his ear with the end of a paper match, looked up sharply.

DeGroot narrowed his eyes. "Of course it was meant for the dog," he said.

"Why 'of course'?"

"Because—"

"Because the dog found it?" Blixen demanded. "The dog was all over the place. The dog could have eaten anything—candy that might have fallen on the floor, scraps in the garbage—"

"A minute ago you had Junkin tossing poisoned meat over the back fence. What happened to that theory?"

"Nothing. Especially if your autopsy finds meat in the dog's stomach."

DeGroot's sarcastic snort brought Dr. Trout to his feet, eyes blazing, face flushed. "Stop that!" the old man bellowed. "Stop it! What's the matter with you!"

Dazed, DeGroot squinted up at the flashing spectacles.

"Man, can't you see his implication?" Trout cried. "Why, it could be anywhere, anywhere, in the salt, the sugar, the flour they cook with." He stared along the counter. "My *God*," he whispered.

DeGroot followed his gaze. "If you mean the poison—" he began, and then stopped.

"He means the poison," Blixen said.

DeGroot moistened his heavy lips.

"Can't you believe it, Teet?" Blixen asked. "Maybe it's because random poisoning to close a restaurant strikes you as a crime, and dirty phone calls never did. Is that possible?"

"It still might have been meant for the dog alone. A poisoned piece of meat . . ."

"It might."

DeGroot put his hands flat on the table and stared at them, then pushed himself to his feet. "I'll have them do the autopsy first thing in the morning," he said.

Trout, who was moving from table to table, shaking salt into the palm of his hand and testing it gingerly on the tip of his tongue, said, "Tonight," when DeGroot passed him.

Massively DeGroot nodded, picked up the telephone.

"Ah, this is no *good*," Trout said in despair, and wiped his salty hand against his trouser leg. "They *will* have to close the place now, there's nothing else for it. Until we find out for sure."

"Someone ought to tell Chavez," Blixen said.

"Have you seen him?"

"He went looking for Isabel. She's back, so I suppose he's out there with her. Out front."

Trout nodded and loped off.

"Yeah, this is DeGroot," DeGroot said into the phone. "Give me the lab, I want to talk to Price." He picked a cigarette out of a pack in his sport-shirt pocket and lighted it, looking blankly over the flame at the cracked window.

Blixen headed for the kitchen, made sure through the little window that there was no one poised on the other side, and pushed open the door.

CHAPTER EIGHT

It was a cluttered, low-ceilinged place, badly planned, with the work counters well away from the refrigerator, and two deep sinks squatting under the windows in the cool half of the room, where the range should have been. The bovine girl, her nose cherry-red from weeping, lay on her side on a canvas cot, stockings twisted, chewing on a handkerchief. She caught sight of Blixen in an ornate mirror that hung in the alcove at the bottom of the stairs and sat up. Her eyes were sick and cornered. "Ray?" she called.

A screen door banged on the back porch.

"Oh, did I startle you?" Blixen asked. "I'm sorry." He smiled. "I'm a friend of Isabel's."

The girl's eyes wavered toward the porch and Blixen turned to see the curly-haired man standing there. He was olive-skinned and handsome, stocky, powerful, dressed in a short-sleeved sweater of horizontal red and white stripes, a pair of flared blue pants, and a knitted black cap, like Jean Gabin in the thirties, like the arrogant lead in a Pagnol movie. "Oh, good evening," Blixen said.

"Hi, sport," said the curly-haired man. The face was Gabin's; the voice was a choirboy's. He stood rubbing a callus on his neck and watching Blixen out of slitted black eyes.

Blixen cleared his throat and glanced back at the girl. "Yes," he said. "Well. You must be Gloria. The cousin. I don't know if Isabel's ever mentioned me. My name's Blixen. We work together."

"You used to work together," the curly-haired man said. "She's through with all that half-assed sham now."

"And you are . . . ?"

"I'm a friend of the family."

"This is my *novio*, Mr. Cabral," Gloria whispered.

"What was it you wanted back here, sport?" Cabral approached on the balls of his feet, loose as a dancer playing the villain. "The kitchen's closed."

"That's what I wanted, in a way," Blixen said.

Cabral cocked his large head. "Oh, right. That's what all you Anglo mothers wanted—in a way—wasn't it? But they didn't do it for you, sport."

"Ray, come on," Gloria said in a hopeless undertone.

"They did it for the dog," Cabral said. "They'll be open again tomorrow."

"I'm afraid they won't."

Cabral twitched an eyebrow. "Who'll stop 'em?"

"The board of health. The police."

"Let's bet," Cabral said.

Timidly Gloria said, "We're getting a Mexican lawyer. Papa just called one."

"I think he'll advise you to cooperate," Blixen said. "Certainly until the strychnine's found."

"Ask Junkin where the strychnine is," Cabral said.

"They will," Blixen said, "as soon as they locate him. In the meantime, it could be anywhere, couldn't it?"

"Not here."

"Why not?"

"No more dogs to kill. He got what he wanted."

"Unless the dog picked it up by mistake."

Gloria pushed her long hair away from her face. "How do you mean by mistake?"

But Cabral understood, and had begun to sway back and forth, like a restive elephant. "By stealing it, he means," he said slowly. "Swiping something off the counter—or . . ." He looked around the kitchen.

The cot crashed against the wall as Gloria leaped to her feet and ran to the drainboard.

"Stay away from there!" Cabral shouted in a piercing tenor.

But she had already opened the soup tureen and lifted the ladle before Blixen could reach her to knock it out of her hand. Her eyes were wild; her fanning hair slapped Blixen's face when she swung to him. "I just took Mama up some of this!"

"Hold her," Cabral grunted, and vanished into the alcove. They could hear him bounding up the stairs, two at a time.

Gloria trembled uncontrollably in Blixen's arms. "Oh, if anything happens to Mama, I'll *die!* Mama's all I've got!"

"Better not let Papa hear that."

The shaking stopped. After a moment Blixen drew back his head. Gloria's fists were clenched against his chest; she was staring at a small garnet ring on her right hand. "No," she said, "no, mustn't forget dear Papa." She stepped sideways, out of his arms, toward the center of the kitchen. "I'm okay now," she muttered. But it was problematical. Her cheeks were ashen; sweat glistened on her forehead and at the base of her throat. She appeared to be listening with all her might for some sound, some word, from upstairs.

The tureen lid had fallen to the floor; Blixen picked it up and put it in the sink. "Did you feed the dog any of this?"

"Yes."

"When?"

"Around five." She stopped. "Or, no . . . I was going to—but it was too hot." She stared at Blixen for a second and then walked rapidly out past the stairs and onto the back porch. Shocked, she pointed at a plastic dish on the flat top of a washing machine. "I *forgot* him!"

The dish was filled with meat ends, vegetable scraps, and the congealing soup.

"It began to thunder," Gloria groaned. "He was so scared of thunder. He wouldn't have eaten anyway. . . ."

Blixen squatted by the two-way dog gate cut into the door beneath the screen. "Would he have gone out?"

But she wasn't listening. Footsteps rattled down the stairs and she swung around to goggle up at Cabral.

"It's all right, no sweat," Cabral said and gathered her clumsily against him. "The soup's safe."

"She'd eaten it?" Blixen asked.

"Not her. She wasn't hungry. The minister's up there—Brouwer— he had a couple of spoonfuls. And Mrs. Bitch ate the rest."

"Don't *call* her that, Ray," Gloria said into his sweater.

"Who's Mrs. Bitch?"

"The Mouth that Walks like a Woman," Cabral said. "Billroth."

"Ray?" Gloria warned.

"You're sure they ate it?" Blixen persisted. "They wouldn't have thrown it out?"

"Billroth wouldn't. She'd eat the plate if somebody'd butter it for her."

"How long ago?"

"Fifteen, twenty minutes. They're both all right."

Gloria had begun to tremble again; Blixen could see the ends of her hair shivering against her blouse. "But then I don't understand," she cried. "What did *Harpo* eat? Everything in the place was in that soup."

"Leftovers?"

"Everything. Wine. Garlic—"

"That's what makes it good, sport," Cabral said. "And anything she'd be afraid to put in, I'd snitch. We don't throw nothing out back here."

Perplexed, Blixen prodded the dog gate with his toe. It flapped freely, noisily. "Gloria tells me Harpo was afraid of thunder."

"Scared to death."

"So he probably wouldn't have gone out after the storm started?"

"He *didn't* go out," Gloria said.

"We'd have seen him," Cabral said. "Or heard him. He didn't go out. We were here all the time."

"Unless he went out the front," Gloria said.

"He never left the restaurant," another voice said. "I can vouch for that."

Wheeling, Blixen smashed his elbow on a cupboard corner and sucked in his breath, eyes squeezed shut.

"Good," Isabel said. "I hope it cripples you."

Cabral guffawed.

"Oh, shut up, Ray," Isabel said glumly. She was standing in the kitchen entrance, one hand on her hip, holding back the door with the other. "Let go of the elbow," she growled at Blixen. "Let the blood circulate."

"Did you hear what happened?" Gloria asked her. "They think Junkin—"

"Yeah, Trout told me."

"There'll have to be an autopsy," Blixen wheezed. "To establish what the dog ate."

Isabel shook her head. "Jesus won't hear of it. They're screaming at each other about that out in the street now. It doesn't matter anyway."

"Certainly it matters!"

"No. I had my eye on the dog every minute. And he didn't eat a thing. He was too nervous. All he could do was drink a little coffee."

"All right, the coffee, then."

"No."

"Isabel!"

"No," Isabel repeated. "It was *my* coffee. I drank it, too." She released the door and drifted back into the restaurant. "And I never felt better in my life, *patrón*," she said over her shoulder.

CHAPTER NINE

She'd nearly reached the end of the long counter before Blixen got himself untracked. He pushed open the swinging door and shouted: "Isabel!" but she sailed ahead as serenely as a deaf-mute and in the next moment was out the front door and gone.

Still cradling his wounded elbow, Blixen strode through the restaurant after her.

The night was villainously cold. Spray off the windswept breakers glittered like sleet in the air. Four men—Trout and Sanderson, Chavez and the sheriff—stood nose to nose in the center of the wet street and argued at the top of their lungs, waving their arms and puffing steam and oaths into one another's faces.

At first he thought she'd escaped him altogether; then she shifted her position and he caught sight of her outlined against one of the parked cars, buttocks propped on a front fender, ankles crossed. She had an unlighted cigarette in her hand and was patting her pants pockets for a match, listening to the street fighters.

Blixen crossed to her and flicked open his lighter.

Isabel glanced up and then threw the cigarette into the street.

"You know, sometimes," Blixen said, "you seem about fifteen years old to me. Then you pull a stunt like that and slip back to your normal twelve."

"Encouraging me to smoke now, are you, *patrón?*"

"Don't call me *patrón*. I don't like it."

"Sorry, *patrón*."

"Aren't you cold?"

"Freezing."

"Come inside."

"Why?"

"I'm afraid you'll catch something."

"I won't. But it wouldn't matter if I did."

"I think you'd find it might matter a great deal if you got laryngitis."

"To who?" Isabel barked. "You?"

"And to you. Have you ever had to loop a full day's work?"

"No. And I never will."

"Stop it."

She swung to him, taut and angry, low-voiced. "You stop it! What's the matter with you? Can't you understand English? I told you I was quitting."

"You can't. You'd be in breach of contract."

"Sue me."

"Isabel," Blixen said, "why are you doing this to yourself? What's the—"

But he'd lost her. She'd crossed her arms, laughing merrily and looking off toward the furious men in the middle of the street. "Listen to that!" she said in delight. "*Ay, que tio!* That sissy Gloria doesn't know how lucky she is. What I'd have given for a father like him!"

"Is that where you learned to act? At your uncle's knee?"

"You think he's acting? Now?"

"Of course."

Isabel pinched her lips between thumb and forefinger, weighing the pros and cons, measuring her uncle's ranting against her own experience. "Well—I agree he's enjoying his rage. . . . But there's a difference."

"What's the difference?"

"Oh, don't be ridiculous, please."

"No, tell me."

She shot him a suspicious glance. "To begin with," she said, "he's not reading someone else's lines. He's pleading a cause he believes in. He's thinking for himself."

"On the contrary," Blixen said, "he's not thinking at all. If he were, he'd be able to see the dead end he's backed himself into."

"What dead end?"

"He won't let DeGroot do an autopsy on the dog."

"You bet he won't. Why should he? Neither would I. There's no law yet that says Anglos can cut up every little—"

"How did the dog die?"

"The dog was poisoned!"

"By whom?"

"Junkin! Or one of his—"

"How?"

"I don't know how! It doesn't make any difference how!"

"How long after you gave Harpo the coffee did you go upstairs, Isabel?"

"Right away."

"And how long after that was it before Harpo died?"

"I don't remember. Quarter of an hour."

"So either he got the strychnine in the coffee—"

"He couldn't have! Why don't you listen? I told you I drank some of it myself, before I gave it to him, and nothing happened."

"Or he found something else on the floor."

"No." Her voice was flat and positive. "I'd cleaned the whole place. There was nothing on the floor."

"Or someone," Blixen continued, "introduced the strychnine into the room after you left. Correct?"

"How would I know? It's your speculation."

"Think it through."

Presently Isabel said: "Impossible. It couldn't have been brought in afterward."

"Why not?"

"Cabral and Gloria were together in the kitchen. Nobody could have sneaked past them."

"So the back was blocked."

"Front and back both. Jesus Mary was out front."

"Maybe," Blixen said.

Isabel's eyebrows rose. "What do you mean maybe? He *said* he was out there."

"Who else said he was out there?"

"He was alone."

"Right," Blixen said. "He was alone."

"Well? So? What's that supposed to signify?"

"To DeGroot?"

"To anybody!"

"To DeGroot," Blixen said, "it might confirm what he's suspected from the start. That Chavez himself poisoned the dog. For its effect on public opinion. To give himself an understandable motive for murder."

Isabel's jaw sagged. "Well, for . . ." She lunged away from the car and erratically started off toward the restaurant. "I don't have to stand here and listen to—" She whirled, came back. "Do you know what you're *saying?*"

"Certainly."

"Do you think my uncle could poison his own *dog?*"

"There's one other explanation," Blixen said.

"*What* explanation?"

"That the dog was never poisoned at all."

Blinking, Isabel said: "But—Dr. Trout—"

"Trout might have been mistaken. It was only a guess on his part."

"A *guess?*" Isabel passed a hand uncertainly across her forehead.

"Suppose, for instance," Blixen resumed, "that Harpo had a fit of some kind. A stroke."

Behind them the four disputants—thumping chests and threatening lawsuits—had pushed one another to the seawall. Isabel stared at the wrathful figure of her uncle and then looked back at Blixen.

"Isabel, wake up," Blixen said. "DeGroot's already convinced himself that Chavez murdered Junkin. He's *half* convinced he poisoned the dog. He'll turn this place upside down looking for a charge to book your uncle on—anything to keep him around. Now if the dog *was* poisoned, an autopsy'll show how and by what and either of those facts might clear Chavez. If he wasn't poisoned, it'll slam *that* door in DeGroot's face. Won't it?"

Isabel shuddered.

"Isabel?"

Gritting her teeth, she said: "But you don't understand. He *hates* autopsies. He'll never—"

"Point out the facts to him. He isn't a fool."

"Couldn't *you* point out the facts?"

"Would he listen to me?"

Isabel slumped, thinking. "No. No." She arched her aching back and stared at the moon for a while, then trudged off toward the ocean and the four men as though weighted down with chains from neck to knees.

From the other side of the shrub behind Blixen, someone murmured: "She looks like a spy going out to the courtyard to be shot, doesn't she?"

Blixen turned.

The round-faced young man in the coonskin cap eased up reluctantly. "Uh—good evening. I don't think we've met. I'm Alfred Brouwer."

"Nils Blixen," Blixen said.

"Right on," Brouwer said, and gave a nervous cough. "Do you think you convinced her?"

"About the autopsy? I hope so."

"So do I. I put in a good word for you, anyway. Little prayer."

"Ah! Well, thank you, Reverend."

"Don't mention it."

"Is that what I call you? Reverend?"

"Or Alfred." Brouwer noticed a loose shoelace and bent to tie it. "With most people it's just Alfred. I must look like an Alfred." He straightened, puffing. "It's this fat face. I'll also look sixteen until I'm sixty, and then everything'll collapse at once, like the one-hoss shay." A light went out in a room over the restaurant, and Brouwer sobered. "Uh-oh, do you think she heard that? What's the matter with me? People are in pain, worried sick, and I stand out here like a laughing jackass."

"Well, I don't know," Blixen said. "I don't think laughter necessarily symbolizes indifference."

"I'm certainly not indifferent," Brouwer mumbled. "It's just that I—can't—I haven't been in the ministry very long, and I—often don't know what to say . . . I sometimes wonder if I give dangerous advice." He slid his eyes away from Blixen's. "I—I—I don't mean *dangerous*." His troubled gaze sought out the figures at the seawall. Quieter now, the four men appeared to be conferring over Isabel like surgeons over a desperate case. "They've got to find out what happened to that dog," Brouwer muttered.

"Yes," Blixen agreed slowly. "Well, they will."

"I know I'll be afraid to eat here until they do. I certainly won't send anyone up from the church again, even for a free meal."

"Reverend," Blixen began, "when you say you gave—"

"Do you suppose she's making any progress?"

After a moment Blixen tried again. "What dangerous advice were you talking about, Mr. Brouwer?"

"I didn't mean dangerous," Brouwer replied. His moon face remained averted.

"Mr. Brouwer," Blixen said, "is George Junkin a parishioner of yours?"

The effect was remarkable. Brouwer stumbled along his whole length, like a dog in its sleep; his mouth puckered babyishly. "*Junkin?*" he cried.

"George Junkin."

"Well, why in the world would you think I was talking about George Junkin? I wasn't, as it happens—"

"I didn't say you were. I asked if he belonged to your church."

"And even if I had been," Brouwer declared, "I wouldn't tell you! I couldn't! Communication in the vestry is as privileged as it is in a lawyer's office!" He attempted to breathe through his nose, to unclench his fists. "More so," he said. He cast a savage look at Blixen, who was blowing into his cupped hands, waiting. Brouwer grabbed off his coonskin cap and swung it by its tail against his leg. "All right, yes, he's a parishioner of mine," he said. "What about it? I don't—"

"I thought you might be able to shed some light on his disappearance."

"We weren't very close."

"What's he like, Reverend?"

"He never blinks. Short man—brown hair—"

"I meant basically. Inwardly."

"Oh. Repressed." Brouwer twisted his furred hat in his hands. "He —asked the bishop to replace me once. I'd only been here a month."

"Replace you why?"

Flushing, Brouwer said: "It's not—it doesn't—well . . . I brought a rock group into the Sunday school. I didn't see why 'Jesus Wants Me for a Sunbeam' shouldn't have a beat. I suppose that was pretty dumb on my part."

"How did the kids react?"

"They loved it."

"Then I should think it was pretty intelligent on your part."

"It wasn't." Brouwer put the hat on again and stood with his hands clasped behind his back. "It got me off on the wrong foot. With the people who counted. That's always been my cross. I act before I think." Secretly his anxious eyes sought the restaurant's darkened window. "I did it again tonight."

"Upstairs?"

"Yes." Then, so low that Blixen could barely hear him, he added: "That's what I meant about dangerous advice."

"Still—people don't have to act on your advice, Reverend, do they?"

"It's different," Brouwer said obstinately, "when it comes from a minister of the gospel. Especially for a woman with faith. Like Mrs. Chavez."

Surprised, Blixen said: "Is Mrs. Chavez a member of your congregation then?"

"Not a member. But she has faith. We talk a lot."

"I hear she isn't feeling well."

"Mrs. Chavez never feels well, Mrs. Chavez enjoys poor health," Brouwer said. He closed his eyes and expelled his breath harshly. At last he said: "Along with acting before I think, you may have noticed that I'm about as charitable as Donald Duck."

"I notice you tend to excoriate yourself for being born human," Blixen said.

Brouwer rubbed his nose, dissatisfied, then shrugged.

"What's wrong with Mrs. Chavez?" Blixen asked.

"Slipped disc, sacroiliac, something of that nature."

"And you think she's feigning?"

"Oh, no, absolutely not."

"Well . . ."

"She can't walk," Brouwer said, "because she's convinced herself that she can't. She's in pain because she wants to be in pain. That's the long and the short of it."

"She gains something from the pain, you mean."

"Of course. She's waited on hand and foot. She's the center of her family's pity and concern. She gains a great deal. But that's on the subconscious level. Consciously, she wants to walk very badly. I tell her to let God in, let God do the healing, have faith. And she *tries* . . ."

"Can she walk at all?"

"She can go to the bathroom if Mrs. Billroth helps her. She can take a few steps by herself. But it's—I guess the pain—" Brouwer shuddered. "If I thought for one minute that I was seriously hurting her—that she—"

"On the other hand," Blixen said, "suppose she *has* to walk some day. Or run. Men who break windows can also set fires."

"Exactly, precisely!" Brouwer cried. "I've said the same thing a dozen times! I've begged them to send her away from here! She'd never have a chance in a fire! Mrs. Billroth lives two doors up the alley. She'd be glad to take her. But Mr. Chavez won't hear of it, won't hear of it! And this is a fort under siege, Mr. Blixen, make no mistake about that. Even tonight there were noises they couldn't explain, somebody out back—"

Ragged footfalls interrupted him as the four fighters and Isabel trooped back to the restaurant like the tag end of a beaten army. Jesus Mary bore the bent, stricken aspect of a mugger's victim; Sanderson and Trout seemed confused. Only DeGroot, beckoning one of his deputies, had come out of the scrap stronger, evidently, than he'd gone in. "There's the body of a poodle on the back porch here," he boomed. "Take it into the lab. Deliver it to Price."

The deputy bobbed his head and trotted around the group toward the restaurant door. He grinned at Blixen and Brouwer and gave them a broad wink when he passed.

Breaking the silence, Isabel said: "Well, that, I guess, is that."

"I'll have a report for all of you in a day or two," DeGroot said. "In the meantime, your place of business stays closed, Chavez, *comprende?*"

The scarred head began to lift; the expression was incredulous.

At once Blixen said: "What the sheriff means, Mr. Chavez, is that he hopes you'll cooperate with the board of health until this mystery has been cleared up. For the sake of your family and friends. So that no one runs the faintest risk of being poisoned. It's unfair, it's difficult, but I'm sure your allies will understand and that they'll all appreciate your position."

Jesus Mary's eyes remained riveted on his.

"Tio, this is Mr. Blixen," Isabel murmured.

At last Jesus Mary snorted, brushed past DeGroot. "I'm going to bed," he said to Isabel, in Spanish. He stumbled, dead tired, on the curb, then caught himself and walked like a torero into the restaurant.

"Stubborn," DeGroot started.

"Hey, gordo-gut," Isabel cut in, "how'd you like a nice big kick right in your little crotch?"

"All right, all right, all right," Blixen said, "let's just—"

"You know what I ought to do with you, young lady?" DeGroot asked.

"Sweetheart, you aren't *capable* of doing anything with me, so stop dreaming," Isabel said.

"Now, babe," Sanderson put in.

"Oh, keep out of it! Nobody—"

"What!" Dr. Trout exclaimed dramatically. "Can this watch of mine be right? Twenty minutes after *twelve?* No wonder I'm so sleepy." He forced an elaborate yawn and beamed around the circle. "Well, if nobody minds, I think I'll just toddle on home . . . Isabel?"

"Go ahead, Doctor. I'll pick up Jude's medicine tomorrow."

"Good night, then. Good night, Mr. Blixen."

"Good night, sir."

"And thank you, Doctor," DeGroot said.

Trout threw him a deprecatory wave and loped off down the sidewalk, into the cold shadows.

"Did he say twenty after *twelve?*" Brouwer asked. "I think we could all use a little—"

"Reverend, before you go," Blixen began.

"Yes!" Brouwer guiltily lurched around to face him.

"About those noises you mentioned . . ."

"Noises?"

"You said there was some commotion out back."

"Oh! Well—"

Isabel frowned. "Do you mean there's been *more* banging?"

"What?" Brouwer asked. "Well, I don't know about *more*. I—they—rather your *aunt* thought she heard someone earlier, out in the garage."

"Oh, that," Isabel said. "My God, when that woman gets her mind set on something, hell or high water couldn't change it."

"Why? What happened?" Blixen inquired.

"Oh, I don't know," Isabel said tiredly. "They were upstairs alone—Enid and tia—and I think the storm had 'em both scared blue. Anyway, they heard something. A tree scraping the house—car backfiring—something. So of course Jude decided we were being attacked."

"What did it sound like to you?"

"Never heard a bloody thing," Isabel said. "David, we were on the phone. Do you remember when Jude thumped?"

"Oh, right."

"When was this?" Blixen wanted to know.

"This was around eight, quarter after eight," Sanderson said.

"Enid thought it might have been a couple of firecrackers," Isabel said, "but Jude was bound and determined it was the garage door. I told her it couldn't have been. I knew the garage was locked."

"Why?" DeGroot demanded.

"Why what?"

"Why would Chavez keep his garage locked?"

"Buddy," Isabel said, "in this red, white, and blue ghetto I'd keep the *toilet* locked if I could! He kept it locked so none of your super-patriots could plant a bomb in it! Why do you *think* he kept it locked!"

DeGroot stared at her and then gave her up, lifted his hands and dropped them distastefully and said to Blixen: "Nils, I'll see you around. I'll call you. Maybe we can have lunch."

"Wait a minute, Teet," Blixen said.

Isabel widened her eyes at Sanderson. "*Teet?*"

Shuffling his feet uncomfortably, Sanderson said: "It's a nickname his brother gave him. Short for Lester."

Isabel put her hands on her hips, studying DeGroot from head to toe.

From somewhere deep in his throat, DeGroot said: "Well?"

"Yeah, it fits," Isabel decided. "You do look like a Teet, man."

"All right, madam, I've taken about all I intend to take from you."

"She apologizes," Blixen said. "What about the noises?"

"Like hell I apologize!"

"Suppose somebody *has* planted a bomb," Blixen said. "They've tried everything else. It's not out of reason. I think you ought to look into it."

"Into what?" DeGroot asked. "A couple of jumpy ladies' imaginations?"

"I do not apologize!" Isabel howled at Sanderson. "Tell them!"

"They know," Sanderson said.

"Besides," DeGroot said, "if the garage door is locked . . ."

"Let's check it," Blixen urged. "What can it hurt to check? You got your way about the dog. Show your goodwill."

"I haven't got any left," DeGroot said. But he rubbed his hand across the back of his neck and muttered to Brouwer: "What did they say it sounded like?"

"A door banging," Brouwer said.

"Are there any other doors back there they could have heard? Unlocked?"

"Well, there's the back screen. But I asked Mrs. Chavez if it had sounded like that, and she gave me a positive no. Then there's the shed . . . I don't know if they keep that locked or not."

"Is the shed locked, Isabel?" Blixen asked.

"What shed?" Isabel asked sullenly.

"The shed, the *shed!*" Blixen snapped. "This could be important, for God's sake! Stop acting for five minutes and help us!"

Isabel jerked her head up like a teased cobra. Brouwer winced. But the anticipated explosion never materialized. Instead Isabel turned her back, staring out over the ocean. "No," she said.

"Not locked?"

"No."

"Let's take a look," Blixen said.

"Where is this thing?" DeGroot asked.

Timidly, Brouwer said: "Well, I could show you—if Isabel—"

"Do as you please. I don't care."

"Yes. All right. It's this way then."

Dodging a little in the deceptive moonlight, scrambling through the puddles, Brouwer led Blixen and DeGroot up the buckled driveway between the restaurant and the hardware store and across a transverse delivery alley in the rear to a warped garage that was not only locked but double locked and chained as well.

"What the blazes is he hiding in there?" DeGroot asked. "The jewels of the Madonna?"

"There's the shed," Brouwer pointed out.

But they couldn't pry DeGroot away from the garage. Nose pressed to the side window, he said: "Brouwer—what are those sacks?"

"Sacks?"

"By the car."

Brouwer cupped his hands around his eyes. "Oh. Is it fertilizer?"

Before DeGroot could respond, a window on the restaurant's second floor banged open and a woman cried loudly: "Who is that? Who's down there?"

She was dressed in a white flannel nightgown; there was a roguish cloche nightcap on her head. Blixen had never seen anyone uglier.

"It's all right, Mrs. Billroth," Brouwer called. "It's just us."

"Who's us?"

"It's the police, madam, go back to bed," DeGroot ordered.

"We're trying to find out what the noise was you heard earlier," Brouwer explained.

"Well, I can tell you what it wasn't, it wasn't the garage. The garage was locked. If it was anything, it was somebody in the shed."

"Madam," DeGroot said, "how long has the garage been kept locked like this?"

"It's always kept locked. Unless Mr. Chavez is using the car."

"And when did he last use the car?"

"Last? Was it this afternoon? This afternoon."

"The garage was open for a while this afternoon?"

"For a little while."

"And were you around here at that time?"

"Oh, I think so. I must have been."

"Did you notice anything unusual?"

"Well . . ."

"Any odor, say?"

The small eyes popped. "Odor!"

"There's a sweetish odor down here somewhere, Mrs. Billroth," DeGroot said. "And I think it's coming from the garage. I think we'd better find out what it is."

And then Blixen smelled it, too, for the first time, faint and corrupt, unmistakable.

Alarmed, Brouwer had commenced to sniff at the crack between the garage doors. "I can't seem to—but then I've had a cold . . ."

Blixen looked off at the small storage shed, squatting separately in the mud, half smashed by the storm. Its door gaped out and away, like a crippled wing; a finger of moonlight touched a black hose lying on top of a mover's lightweight barrel.

DeGroot and the woman were arguing over what to do next, whether or not to disturb Jesus Mary, who was asleep. Brouwer continued to sniff around the garage. Blixen walked to the shed.

The scent violated his nostrils. He breathed through his mouth as he removed the cold hose from the barrel and lifted the lid.

Behind him, the din of the argument had attracted Isabel and Sanderson to the backyard, and DeGroot turned his attention at once from Mrs. Billroth to the newcomers. He declared in impassioned tones that he'd taken all the obstruction he meant to take and that either they'd open the garage for him or he'd break the door in. If they had nothing to hide, they had nothing to fear.

"Nobody's got anything to hide now, Teet," Blixen said dully. "I can promise you that. Here's what you're looking for."

DeGroot whirled. "Junkin?"

"Maybe."

"Let me see," Isabel cried.

"David, keep her back!" Blixen shouted, and finally managed to force his sick eyes away from the barrel. "You don't want to look," he told them. "There's no head. . . . They've cut the head off. . . ."

CHAPTER TEN

He dreamed he was alone on a rusted ship, plowing through slabs of green water toward a port he was afraid to visit. He needed to relieve himself—his bladder ached—but there was no lavatory aboard and he understood that he mustn't pollute the ocean. He was desperate to learn the time. He set himself to count the ship's bells. Five—

Galvanized, he flapped awake, fumbling for the telephone, shouting, "Hello, hello!" even before he'd got the receiver to his ear.

"Hello!" his secretary shouted back. "Hello!"

"*Hello,*" Blixen said.

"Who *is* this?" Miss Firebush bawled fiercely.

"Muriel, for Christ's sake, who do you think it is?" Blixen ground out. "It's me. You placed the call. Who did you expect?"

"Well, you took me aback," Miss Firebush said. "I was about to hang up and then you came on, just screaming."

"I was having a nightmare." Blixen propped himself on an elbow. His watch was missing from its usual place on the bedside table. He'd put it in the bathroom, he remembered, when its ticking had threatened to unhinge him. "What time is it?"

"It's five past eleven," said Miss Firebush. "You had appointments at nine-thirty, ten-fifteen, and eleven. You're also going to miss dailies."

"I'll see dailies later."

"And Mr. Todd wants to talk to you the minute you get in."

"I'll bet he does. Was it in the paper?"

"Was what in the paper?"

"The body we found. In Oceanport."

"You mean the headless thing?" Miss Firebush gasped. "*You* found that? It didn't mention your name."

"Or Isabel's?"

"No. Just that this naked corpse was in this mover's barrel with its head and hands cut off. They don't even seem to know who he is. Was."

"No, they don't. Not yet."

"Mercy," Miss Firebush said.

"I'll tell you what you'd better do," Blixen said. "Call Publicity and have them send somebody down to talk to Isabel, handle the press—"

"What's Isabel got to do with it?"

"Nothing. She was just there. I don't want her pestered and I don't want her hurt. She's at the Cucaracha Mexican restaurant on A Street in Oceanport."

"Did she see this thing? Isabel?"

"No, thank God."

"What was it like?" Miss Firebush made a gurgling sound. "Wait, don't tell me."

"No way," Blixen said.

"No wonder you were having nightmares. Was it after you?"

"The dream didn't have anything to do with that," Blixen said. "I seemed to be on this ship—all alone . . ."

"Naturally. No crew."

"What?"

"You were on a ship without hands."

Blixen sat back against his pillow, astounded, conscious again of the pressure on his bladder and the lack of a lavatory on the dream boat. Without hands—and without a head. "Muriel, the mind's a fantastic instrument," he said. "The puns it makes. The puns."

"Yes," Miss Firebush said vaguely. "Oh. Mr. Loos called."

"Who?"

"Bernie Loos."

Barney Lewis was his associate producer, a heavyset, dogged ex-actor who kept the technical wheels of the organization oiled. "Yes? Well?"

"He's dubbing today and he has to know if you want to check each reel separately or do you want to wait for the whole picture or what?"

"Tell him I'll wait."

"And Mr. Carpalos came by and says he absolutely has to see you because he's got a crisis."

"Mr. Kapralos always has a crisis," Blixen said. "Nothing has gone right for Mr. Kapralos since Edison invented the kinetoscope."

"I guess not."

"Tell him I'll look in this afternoon."

"Are you coming right over?"

"As soon as I phone a couple of people."

"I think I'll go to lunch a little early then."

"Do that."

"Bye-bye."

Bemused, still mulling over the word tricks his mind had played in his dream, Blixen went to the bathroom, shaved, dressed, opened the curtains, and dialed Sanderson. After the storm, the dark blue skies were scrubbed and sparkling. There was no place under skies like that for murders or headless corpses. It was a day, Blixen thought, out of the 1940s, as clean as every day had been when he was sixteen, fresh from the chilled Northwest, stunned by the extent of the town, twitching with lust for the usherettes at Grauman's. There'd never been a morning without a skywriter, nor a night without a major-studio preview. Everything had been surprising then. He'd seen Rita Hayworth in the Brown Derby . . .

"Hello," Sanderson said groggily.

"David? Nils."

"Oh . . ."

"Are you awake?"

"Keep talking. I'll find you."

"What time did you get in?"

"Ten minutes to six."

"Good. You've had more than five hours' sleep. That ought to be enough for a virile young stud like yourself."

"It should, shouldn't it," Sanderson said. "I wonder why it isn't. Maybe I'm running down."

"Where's Isabel?"

"Still at the beach. I tried to persuade her to come back with me, but she wouldn't."

"Staying with the family?"

"No, there's no room. Mrs. Billroth decided to sleep with the aunt last night, so Jesus used the cot downstairs and Gloria and Isabel are in Mrs. Billroth's apartment."

"I'm surprised you came home yourself, David."

"Well, I have to rewrite the rest of this lousy script. I wanted to talk to you about that. I thought I might be able to switch most of

Isabel's lines in the nightclub scene to the cigarette girl. Do you recall that part?"

"Yes."

"What do you think?"

"You'll have to do a little juggling," Blixen warned. "But if she isn't going to be available, I don't suppose we have any choice."

"I don't suppose so." Sanderson hesitated. "Nils—don't give up on her."

"Don't worry about it."

"I can't find out exactly what her problem is. But she'd go crazy if she couldn't act."

"I know."

"She'll be back next season."

"Of course she will." Neither of them, Blixen noticed, said what both of them must have been thinking. *If* there was a next season. "What happened down there after I left?"

"Nothing much. They took the body away, searched the house, garage, the grounds. . . ."

"Find any clothes? Any identification?"

"Nothing."

"Blood?"

"No."

"What does Mrs. Junkin say?"

"She's too hysterical to look at the remains."

"I don't blame her."

"God, neither do I."

"David," Blixen said, and stopped.

"Yes? What?"

"David—could I ask a favor of you?"

"Certainly."

"Let *me* rewrite the nightclub scene," Blixen said. "I'd—really rather have you back in Oceanport, with Isabel."

"Why?"

"I don't know why."

At last Sanderson said: "Well, sure, Nils. All right."

"Maybe it's because I can't imagine any logical reason on earth for anybody to put that body in Jesus Mary's shed. Unless it's part of the whole pattern . . ."

"Of trying to drive Jesus Mary away?"

"A dead rat on the doorstep," Blixen said, "a dead dog in the kitchen, a dead man outside—"

"Um," Sanderson said. "Yes. What's next, dead member of the family?"

"Don't scare our girl. Just keep an eye on her."

"Yes. I will."

"And get her away from there if you can."

"Oh, I will, I will."

"I'll try to make it down tonight."

"See you then."

"Goodbye, David."

"Goodbye, Nils."

After he'd hung up, Blixen brewed himself a cup of coffee and then called the Ramona County sheriff's office.

Deputy Fry, the night switchboard man, had given way to a young lady with a dapper, tailored voice, who put him through to DeGroot the moment he stated his business.

"Yeah, Nils," DeGroot said. He sounded badgered and elderly, under hair-trigger control.

"Good morning," Blixen said. "What's happening?"

"Oh, nothing," DeGroot said. "I'm just sitting here eating gumdrops and watching TV, bored as hell. What do you mean *what's happening?*"

"Have you identified your corpse yet?"

"Not yet. We will."

"Do you still think it's Junkin?"

"It's Junkin. It's the right height, the right weight, right coloring."

"How long had he been dead?"

"Since Saturday. Isn't that the oddest coincidence?"

"I have a feeling you're trying to tell me something, Teet."

"You do, do you?"

"So Jesus Mary shot his man in the head," Blixen went on, "and then cut it off so you couldn't find the bullet, right?"

"For that, and to muddy the identification process."

"I imagine that's why he took the hands, too."

"Can you think of a better reason?"

"I'm so dumb," Blixen said, "I can't even think of a reason why he'd leave the rest of the body. Surely Mrs. Junkin ought to be able to recognize her husband even without the head and the hands."

"I'd think so. If we can ever get her down here."

"And even if she can't, there must be medical records, X rays, scars . . ."

"There must be."

"All right, then, if there are scars, he really failed to destroy identification, didn't he? Why do you suppose he left the legs on, Teet?"

"I suppose," DeGroot said, "that he was interrupted in his butchery."

"I see. And where was that?"

"What?"

"Where did he do this butchering? In the shed?"

"You know it wasn't in the shed. You saw the shed. There was no blood on the floor. As a matter of fact, there was very little blood anywhere. The body had been drained white before it was put in the barrel."

"So," Blixen said, "Jesus Mary killed his man somewhere else—"

"Yes."

"Butchered him—"

"Yes."

"And then carried the corpse back to his own place, stuffed it into a barrel, and put the whole business in an unlocked shed where anybody could stumble over it at any time."

"Yes," DeGroot said.

"Teet . . ." Blixen murmured in disappointment.

"I'll even tell you his thinking when he did it," DeGroot said. "He *wanted* the body discovered there. To tie in with the rest of this imaginary persecution."

"Imaginary?"

"We've put a tap on his phone. With his permission. We've got a plainclothes detail watching his restaurant night and day. And there hasn't been an off-color remark or a hint of vandalism since we got there."

"You wouldn't expect the bigots to pull their horns in after all the publicity?"

"I'd expect Chavez himself to lay low knowing half the police in Ramona County had their eye on him," DeGroot said.

"I see."

"No, you don't. You're crying too hard for the downtrodden minority. Well, maybe you ought to save a tear for the downtrodden majority. Especially after an operator like this gets through with 'em."

"Now let's see if I've got it all straight," Blixen said. "He breaks his own windows, he sends himself obscene letters and phone calls, he butchers his next-door neighbor—"

"Poisons his dog."

"Poisons his dog," Blixen echoed. "How'd he do that, by the way?"

"Probably fed it pure strychnine, out of his hand. The autopsy showed the dog hadn't taken any solid food for twelve hours or more."

Blixen frowned. "For— Are you sure?"

"Of what? The autopsy report? Certainly."

Lowering his cup, Blixen said: "What about coffee?"

"Yes, the dog had ingested a large amount of coffee."

"But nothing else?"

"Nothing else."

"Well."

"Puts a certain unkind pressure on our little Mexican friends, doesn't it, Nils," DeGroot said. "Either Jesus Mary fed the dog strychnine when Isabel went upstairs, or it was in the coffee and Isabel lied about drinking it herself." He sighed. "Pretty problem," he said.

CHAPTER ELEVEN

It was, Blixen admitted on his way to work, a very pretty problem indeed. He sat in the back of the cab, depressed and impassive, until they jolted to a stop and he saw that they were at the studio gate. He rolled down his window. "Jim," he greeted the young guard on duty. "Little late today."

"I'm surprised you're in at all, after Oceanport," the guard said.

"I see Muriel's made the rounds."

"She wanted me to remind you that Mr. Todd's waiting."

"I know."

"Boy, that must have been some experience," the guard said. "Oceanport."

"Terrible, terrible," Blixen said.

"Oh—and Muriel told me to tell you a Mr. Shiva or something like that was on the lot, looking for you. He went down to the set."

"Shiva," Blixen said.

"Shiver? Shaver?"

"Schreiber?" Blixen asked.

"It might have been Schreiber. You know Muriel."

Blixen glanced at his watch. "Where are we?"

The guard consulted a production schedule. "Uh—*Stagg* Company—lagoon."

"Left at the corner," Blixen informed the cab driver, "then straight ahead as far as you can go, and right at the fence."

The driver nodded.

"Wait!" Blixen said. He stuck his head out the window. "Oh, Jim?"

The guard, who had gone back into his booth to check off Blixen's name, came out again curiously.

"Jim," Blixen continued, "you were a pre-med student—"

"Four bloody years."

"What's strychnine?"

"*What* is it? It's an alkaloid—systemic poison."

"A powder?"

"Comes in crystals—colorless—extremely bitter."

"Would it take less to kill a dog, say, than a human being?"

"Wouldn't take much to kill either one."

"Are human beings ever immune to it?"

"Immune? No! *Strychnine?*"

"I thought I read somewhere that you could build up an immunity by taking a little each day and then—"

"Well, they used to say that about arsenic. I'm not sure it's true. . . ."

"Arsenic, of course," Blixen said. "Arsenic." He let his chin sink onto his chest, brooding. "So if there was strychnine in a cup of coffee, and a dog and a human both drank out of it, you'd expect them both to die?"

"Die or be pretty sick, depending on the dose," said the guard.

Blixen studied him for a moment more, then nodded and said: "Thanks, Jim."

He leaned back in the seat and watched the studio streets and the brown, elephantine sound stages slip past. They drove through a Norman village and across a New England square, where a number of pilgrims were playing bridge on a rustic gallows, and then followed a rutted wagon track down to a Tahitian lagoon, which had been redressed for this production to resemble a private bay on Lake Tahoe. Flat silver reflectors gleamed in the sun. A tall man sat on the end of his spine in a canvas chair marked DIRECTOR with a white handkerchief tied over his bald head, asleep. On a rotting pier two stuntmen—representing Murf Smith and the psychotic villain he'd cornered here—plotted their moves for the camera crew like ballet masters, gouging and grunting and cartwheeling over and over in a ritual as stylized as Kabuki.

"*This* is how you make movies?" the cab driver asked.

"This is how," Blixen replied.

The driver opened Blixen's door, looking at the extras dozing in the shade and the knitting wardrobe women and the grips horsing around on the bank. "Don't anybody ever work?"

"Believe it or not, they *are* working," Blixen said. "It's like the Army. You hurry up to wait."

"Huh," said the driver. "About how much do these guys shoot a day?"

"Oh—they'll get three, three and a half pages on location. Say two minutes of finished film."

"Two *minutes!* For all *day?*"

"Eight to six," Blixen said.

"Mother of God," said the cab driver.

Face frustrated, staggered by the indolence, he clambered back into the cab, slammed his door, and rattled off.

"What did you do, refuse to tip him?" Donald Gould called. The old English actor, who played Stagg's best friend, had unbuttoned his vicar's collar and was drinking a beer under a bush.

Smiling, Blixen walked over. "No, he's mad at the industry. He thinks you all ought to work harder."

"Chap's missed his calling," Gould said. "He should have been a producer, eh?"

"No question about it."

"We're a little behind here at that," Gould said.

"What's the problem?"

"I'm not sure. It would have gone faster with Isabel aboard. This director prepares awfully thoroughly, I find. Of course he had to change his setups, switch everything around. I expect it unnerved him."

"Is he all right now?"

"Oh, I think so, yes," Gould said. "Actually, I missed Isabel myself. I play better to her reactions. She stirs me somehow. Well, she'll be back tomorrow."

"I'm afraid she won't."

Gould paused with the beer can halfway to his lips. "She won't?" He lowered the can. "Why on earth not?"

"Isabel," Blixen said, "seems to be going through some kind of an emotional crisis, Donald. I don't pretend to understand it. I do know it's serious. And now, on top of everything else, she's involved in the Oceanport business."

"What Oceanport—" Gould stiffened. "Not the murder! That headless horror?"

Blixen nodded.

"Lord," Gould murmured. "Well, well, well." He swallowed the rest of the beer quickly. "Involved how?"

"The body was found on her uncle's property."

"This is the uncle who has the restaurant—Jesus Mary?"

"Yes."

"Yes, she's awfully keen on that man," Gould said. "Terribly keen. . . . Well, he didn't do it or anything, did he?"

"No."

"Thank God for that at least." Gould absently crushed the beer can between his thin hands.

On the pier, the stuntmen flailed and grimaced in slow, measured movements.

"Donald," Blixen said, "you and Isabel got to be fairly good friends during this past season, didn't you?"

"Fairly, yes. Why?"

"Why is she so keen on Jesus Mary?"

"Well, he's certainly a surrogate father, isn't he."

"What happened to her own father?"

"Dead."

"When? How?"

Gould glanced at him uncomfortably, then tossed the flattened beer can into a nearby litter basket. "She's very sensitive about it, Nils," he said. "I'm not sure I have the right to tell you." He took a deep breath. "Well. He was shot in a holdup."

"In Mexico?"

"In Texas. Isabel was twelve. She'd always loved to act and luckily she was excellent at it. She got a job in a local radio station just about the time her father lost *his* job, so the family could go on eating, at least. And she did splendidly. It was a soap-opera thing and they kept building her part until she was the virtual star of it. Then—about six months later—the police called and said they'd surprised her father attempting to hold up a gasoline station and they'd killed him."

Mutely Blixen shook his head.

"Dreadful story," Gould agreed. "She's had quite a life, that young woman. . . . Anyway, the uncle stepped right in, filled the gap as well as he could, saw her through school, college—"

"Oh, Nils!" someone hollered.

Shading his eyes, Blixen was finally able to spot Wade Schreiber on top of a knoll beside the sound truck. Spaniel-eyed and small, thick military mustache bouncing in the breeze, Schreiber trotted toward him.

"Well, Donald," Blixen said, "thanks very much."

"I presume she'd like you to keep that particular story confidential, Nils," Gould said.

"I will."

"Give her my love."

Blixen waved his assent and moved across the meadow to meet his lawyer.

Puffing, Schreiber pumped his hand and fought to catch his breath. "Look at this," he said. "Thirty-three years old and I'm ready for the junk heap. I'd join a gym if I thought I could pass the entrance exam."

"Too many late hours, Wade."

"I knew you'd throw that up to me. That was the first weeknight I've spent away from the house in four years. The babysitter said she thought you'd left a message, but she couldn't remember it."

"No, I just gave my name."

"Well, she said you sounded agitated. I must have called your apartment every hour on the hour from eleven until three."

"I was in Oceanport."

"Muriel told me. Are you in trouble?"

"Not with the law."

"Is Isabel?"

"Not yet. It's Isabel's uncle I'm concerned about."

"Chavez, yes—the Communist."

Irritably Blixen said: "Now who identified him that way?"

"Unimpeachable source," Schreiber replied. "According to the paper."

"Did they quote DeGroot?"

"DeGroot . . . oh, the sheriff. Yes, they did."

"There's your unimpeachable source," Blixen said.

"DeGroot thinks Chavez did the killing?"

"He's convinced of it."

"Sorry to hear *that,*" Schreiber said.

"He was convinced of it," Blixen added, "before we even found the body."

"What do you think?"

"I think Chavez was probably capable of killing the man who was trying to drive him out of town, a neighbor named Junkin, but I don't think it was Junkin in the barrel."

"But DeGroot does?"

"Yes."

"Why? The paper said there was no way to identify the corpse."

"Sheriff's intuition."

"I see." Schreiber rubbed a knuckle over his huge mustache. "I hope, Nils, that your own staunch belief isn't based on friend's intuition."

"I'm afraid it is, partly. On that—and a reaction I got from Junkin's minister when I probed a little too deep." Blixen studied the wild flowers on the hill, ordering his thoughts. "He'd been talking about a minister's responsibility in giving advice, the dangers in that. . . . Well, I'd already gained a certain impression of Junkin from his doctor, and even from DeGroot. I knew that Junkin was fifty, highly repressed, married to an unappetizing wife, strongly pro-establishment. . . . I thought if that man ever found himself on the edge of a breakdown, he'd be bound to consult God first. So I asked Brouwer—the minister—if he had."

"And Brouwer denied it?"

"Like a skyrocket going off."

"How about that."

"It occurred to me," Blixen said, "that God might have inspired Brouwer to give some eminently sensible advice—that he might have told Junkin to let go a little, live a little before it was too late."

"What kind of a minister *is* this?"

"The kind to bring a rock group into Sunday school."

"Ho ho *ho*," Schreiber said.

"Then, of course," Blixen went on, "if Junkin was wise enough to listen to God's counsel, and to take off one Saturday afternoon for Mexico or Canada or the South Seas, the second thoughts on Brouwer's part might have been fairly pungent."

"Might they not, might they not, indeed . . ." Schreiber gnawed at his mustache. "So you want—what? Junkin traced?"

"If you can."

"What about photographs? I'll be using Pep Cisneros."

"Junkin was prominent in Oceanport. Tell Pep to try the newspaper morgue."

"Who did Junkin see last?"

"He had an appointment with a lawyer in San Diego named Hopkins, but he never showed up."

"Oh, I know Curtis Hopkins," Schreiber said. "I'll call Curtis."

"Good luck, Wade."

"You know, one other thought occurs to me," Schreiber said, "as I'm sure it must have to you. If Junkin isn't the corpse, he might very well be the murderer."

"Yes, he might."

"Perfect way to embarrass his old Communist enemy before he left."

"Yes."

"He might have found a body on the beach—a tramp—drowned—"

"Then why cut off the head and the hands?" Blixen asked.

"Oh—to avoid identification—I don't know."

"Why would anyone want to hide the identity of a tramp?"

"*Well.*" Schreiber looked confused. "It was just a casual thought, Nils. I—"

"No. It isn't at all casual. It's the key to the whole case."

Schreiber sighed and pressed down the hair on the crown of his head.

"Let's take it step by step," Blixen said. "First, a body is placed in Jesus Mary's shed. Why?"

"To embarrass Jesus Mary."

"Second, this body is mutilated in a particularly abhorrent manner. Why?"

"So that no one will recognize it."

"Why?" Blixen asked.

Schreiber stared at him like an intelligent chimpanzee wondering which button to press to earn the banana.

"All right, here's Junkin—or anyone else—walking along the beach," Blixen said. "He sees a dead stranger. He decides to play a trick on Jesus Mary. So he cuts off the stranger's head and his hands."

"No, he doesn't," Schreiber said softly.

"Why not?"

Triumphantly Schreiber said: "Because no one could have linked him to the stranger anyway. Even if the stranger hadn't been drowned to begin with. Even if Junkin had murdered him."

"Right," Blixen said.

"So there was no stranger," Schreiber said.

"No stranger, right again," Blixen said.

Excitedly Schreiber said: "So, then, wait a minute, wait a minute, your hunch that it also couldn't be Junkin is absolutely correct! Because the killer would *want* Junkin to be recognized—to fix the crime as firmly as he could on Jesus Mary!"

"Unless DeGroot's correct," Blixen amended, "and Jesus Mary did the killing."

"Do you believe that?"

"Not for a minute."

"There you are," Schreiber said. He continued to press at the crown of his head, and a cowlick there continued to spring vigorously back between pressings. "Although I'm blessed if I can see how this gets us any forrader," he said.

"It defines our goals. The crucial thing now is to establish the identity of that corpse."

"I see . . . Why?"

"Because there might be a visible connection between corpse and murderer. *Some* connection, no matter how slight."

"Of course." Schreiber sighed. "Okay, I'll get Pep started on the Junkin trace this afternoon."

"Thanks, Wade."

"Look out, here comes your friend."

"Which friend?"

"Kapralos. I saw him down by the lake a few minutes ago. I thought he was about to jump in."

Blixen followed Schreiber's nod. A bowed figure in decent black, face as pale as a tormented saint's, was laboring up the slope toward them. "That's his happy expression," Blixen said. "Wait until you catch Socrates depressed."

Schreiber laughed and gripped Blixen's upper arm. "Keep in touch, Nils, will you? I'll call you as soon as Pep has anything at all."

"Fine. Give Pep my best."

Schreiber left thoughtfully, his hands in his pockets. At the same time, wheezing like a broken concertina, Kapralos came to rest. He watched Schreiber head up the rutted track and then looked morosely at Blixen. "I've been trying to find you everywhere."

"Yes, well, here I finally am."

"We're in trouble."

"Of course we're in trouble. We're always in trouble. Who's done what to us this time?"

"I really don't know where to start," Kapralos said. He brought his cupped hand down over his mouth and absently stared off into the distance. "Tomorrow's location's gone. I'll begin there."

Presently Blixen said: "I don't quite grasp what you mean by gone."

"Gone," Kapralos said. "Exploded. Blown up."

"Blown up," Blixen repeated.

"The Red Baron Company needed a French farmhouse for a Spad

to dive into, so somebody told them to take our cabin. They said we wouldn't be needing it."

"I can't believe this. . . ."

"Apparently there was a breakdown in communications somewhere."

"I cannot *believe* this!" Blixen shouted. "Even for this studio, that's—" Below him, the script clerk was listening avidly. "Can we bring 'em inside?"

"No. The library set won't be finished until Friday."

"Then we'll play it in the woods."

But Kapralos was shaking his head again.

"What?" Blixen shouted. *"No?* For Christ's sake, they haven't burnt the *woods* down?"

"It's not the woods. It's the rewriting. Sanderson isn't in and nobody answers at his apartment."

"That's all right, never mind about Sanderson, I'll rewrite it myself."

"I don't know what to advise you about Isabel, then," Kapralos said, "whether to leave her in or take her out."

"She'll be out. Definitely."

"Well—does Mr. Todd know about that?"

"Not yet."

"I think you'd better tell him."

"When I get a minute."

"Maybe you'd better find a minute," Kapralos said.

"Socrates—"

"He just asked me to call her agent," Kapralos said, "and inform him that we'd start breach of contract proceedings if Isabel wasn't on the set and ready to work at eight o'clock tomorrow morning."

After a time, Blixen murmured: "And did you do that?"

"Yes, I did," Kapralos said. "I mean, the man's the head of the studio. I tried to suggest that it might be better if he waited to talk to you first, but he said he hadn't been able to reach you and he was at his wit's end trying to find a way to get you to come to his office."

"He found one," Blixen said.

CHAPTER TWELVE

"What joke?" Arthur Todd asked. Stuffed into his swivel chair behind his curved captain's desk, resembling an Edwardian yachtsman in ice-cream colored pants and a blue blazer, he watched Blixen out of hooded poker-player eyes. The thick linen curtains on his office windows gave the room an undersea tint, greenish and drowned; in their lighted wall boxes, his model sloops and whalers seemed to dig through olive oceans.

"Arthur," Blixen began, and halted.

Todd never had been more gracious and interested. "Yes, boy?"

At last Blixen forced himself out of the fat leather chair and walked to the door and back to stretch his legs, to calm his mind. "Arthur, let me see if I can clarify my position here," he said. "To begin with, if I thought for one second that you were serious about this suit, I'd never have come by." He paused at the desk. "I'd have called your analyst."

"*Would* you."

"We've worked together too long, I think. Our problem is that we know each other's moves too well."

"So you decided that I wasn't daffy, I was just foolin'."

"That's what I decided."

"Why?" Todd murmured.

Blixen reseated himself. "Tell me how this studio intends to sue an unsigned player for breach of contract?"

"Oh, I think you'll find that Isabel Chavez has a legal contract."

"She has a legal contract," Blixen said, "with NFB Productions, not with this studio."

"Correct," Todd admitted.

Blixen waited.

"But that won't matter, will it, boy," Todd continued. "Since *you'll* be bringing the suit."

"What's your analyst's number, Art?" Blixen asked.

Todd's laughter rumbled in his chest. "You mean you won't bring the suit?"

"That's what I mean. I won't bring the suit."

"In other words," Todd said, "you, the president of NFB Productions, are now telling me to my face that you have no intention of living up to your own contract with this studio."

"My contract," Blixen said, "calls for me to produce *Stagg at Bay—*"

"Using your best abilities, talents and judgments," Todd put in.

"Ah," Blixen said, "so we're leading up to judgments, are we?"

"You bet we're leading up to judgments." Todd jerked open a desk drawer and pulled out a sheaf of papers. "National Nielsens, week ending November 18—*Stagg at Bay*—in an episode without Isabel Chavez—down two share points from its seasonal average. Second episode without Isabel Chavez—week of December 16—down *four* share points!" He threw the papers back in the drawer and slammed it shut. "Now you clear your ears out, boy, and you listen to me. That show's fighting for its goddamn life. It needs every share point it can find, anywhere it can find 'em. Which means it needs Isabel Chavez. Don't ask me why. I think she looks like something a gang rape would turn away from in horror, but the public likes her and the network likes her and that's what matters. You follow me so far?"

"I've lapped you twice, Art."

"Yeah, maybe, maybe. And maybe not. What I'm trying to point out to you, my friend, is that you cannot *afford* to leave that kid out of your last two episodes, you cannot *afford* it!"

"That woman is in serious emotional—"

"Ah, serious my ass!" Todd snapped. "There ain't an actress alive who's over four years old emotionally. She's throwing a temper tantrum, and either you spank her bottom and get her back on the set by eight o'clock tomorrow, or you tell your lawyer to see my lawyer, okay?"

Blixen slapped the arms of his chair and rose to his feet. "Okay," he said. "My lawyer's Wade Schreiber." He started toward the door. "I'll have Wade set up an appointment with the studio attorneys at—"

"Nils!"

Blixen glanced back with his hand on the knob.

"Jesus, boy," Todd whispered, "when it comes to negotiations, you are really a pain in the butt. All I'm asking for is a little sane cooperation."

"No," Blixen said. "All you're asking is for me to try to force a distraught woman to turn her back on the gravest emotional crisis of her lifetime to come into this lunatic asylum and read lines like: 'But, Saul, how did you *know* he'd hidden the money in the hamburger?'" Blixen snorted. "You wouldn't do it, neither would I, and neither will she."

"Even if it means the end of the series?"

"No matter what it means."

Todd swung around in his chair to gaze at the seafaring accounts in his bookcase.

"Well," Blixen said.

"Wait," Todd said. He closed his eyes. "Maybe there's another way."

"Not if it involves Isabel."

"It involves you." Turning back, Todd hoisted himself heavily out of the chair. "I want you to come to New York with me," he said. "For the selling season."

Slowly Blixen closed the office door again.

"It wouldn't be for the whole time," Todd said. "Just for two days. Just long enough to talk to the programming men and Seacliff and the chairman of the board."

Presently Blixen said: "Arthur, I can't leave right now, you know that."

"Why not? I'm taking off tonight. You could fly in after work Wednesday, be back Saturday. My girl'll make all your reservations. The series isn't going to collapse in two days."

"I'm not afraid of the series collapsing."

"Then join me. Let Seacliff understand how much this show means to us. You're the one he'll want to talk to anyway. After that little misunderstanding at my place—"

"There was no misunderstanding."

"Goddamn it, there was a misunderstanding!" Todd bellowed. "*Bend* a little! Is it going to kill you to promise to take the violence out? All right, so there's no violence. Makes it all the easier, don't it? Tell 'em what they want to hear. It's all baloney, but they eat it up. You tell 'em you'll give 'em better stories and bigger guest stars and further locations, and I'll tell 'em I'll up the budget, and by God, who knows, we might pull this disaster out of the fire yet, boy, right?"

Blixen stared at the seafoam-colored area rug for a time and then nodded. "All right, Arthur. Wednesday. Which hotel?"

"Warwick."

"I'll be there."

Todd threw an arm around Blixen's shoulders. "I knew we'd get on the same beam eventually, Nils. We always do. We'd be fools to come to blows over any actress as ugly as that one." He grimaced his puzzlement. "I wonder whatever happened to all the pretty leading ladies," he asked, "like Loretta Young?"

CHAPTER THIRTEEN

Miss Firebush, huddled over the register in Blixen's stifling outer office, clutched her scarf more closely around her freshly set gray hair and said: "Well, howdy, stranger, I began to wonder if you'd gotten lost. Talk about bankers' hours." She gave a whoop of frightened laughter and sat down abruptly at her desk, breathing hard.

"That's a canard about bankers," Blixen said. "Bankers work their tails off."

"Oh," Miss Firebush said. "Well . . ."

"Has Barney called?"

"Barney?"

"Barney Lewis. From the dubbing stage."

"Oh, *Bernie*."

"Bernie, Bernie," Blixen said.

"No, he hasn't. He said he'd give you a ring when he was on the last reel."

"I don't want to talk to anybody else," Blixen said, "unless it's about Oceanport. I'll be rewriting all afternoon." He looked back. "I'd like a cup of coffee, if there's any left, and I'll need a script."

"Yes!"

The heat in his own office had been raised to its maximum, and as always Blixen turned it off and stopped by the seven-foot-tall philodendron plant near his desk to see how wilted it was, but Miss Firebush had thoughtfully watered it and it looked as bright and tough as a jungle vine. His desk was clear except for a list of late phone messages lying across his herd of ceramic hippos. Three from Todd's office, one from Kapralos, one from Schreiber. He crumpled the list and tossed it into the waste basket and sat pensively rearranging his hippos into a straggling nose-to-tail line from the desk calendar to the ashtray, and finally, when he realized how still it was outside, he got up and crossed to his door and looked out at Miss Firebush, who was seated at her desk with her finger to her nose.

"Muriel?" he said.

Miss Firebush leaped convulsively and threw him a tortured grin. "Yes, sir!" she said.

"Can't you find the script?"

"Well," said Miss Firebush, "to tell you the truth, I'm really not sure which script you want."

"I see," Blixen said. "It's the current one."

"Ah."

"And you may as well bring along the last one, too. The one we're shooting last."

"Yes."

"Thank you."

Reflectively Blixen returned to his desk and toyed with his hippos until Miss Firebush lugged the two scripts and his coffee in and placed it all with a flourish on the blotter before him.

"*There* we are," she said. "I'm awfully sorry I took so long. I don't know where my head is today."

"Perfectly all right."

"Well . . ."

"Muriel," Blixen said, "are you afraid of me?"

Miss Firebush, shuddering to a stop as though her brakes had locked, said: "*Afraid* of you! Afraid of *you?*" She laid a hand on her flushed upper chest and laughed uproariously. "Oh, my," she gasped. "My. My."

"Sit down, Muriel," Blixen said. "Close the door. Please."

Miss Firebush stared at the knob for a second, then banged the door shut and dropped like a stone onto the sofa. She leaned forward, knees together, back rigid, hands squeezed white around a dictation book, smiling desperately at him.

"Let's see," Blixen said, "we've been working together now since —when? Last June?"

"Has it been that long?" Miss Firebush exclaimed. "For heaven's sake. Well—that's really quite a while for a replacement girl, isn't it?"

Blixen, sipping at the coffee, looked up. "For a what?" he asked.

"Replacement girl. I replaced your permanent secretary last year when she—"

"Muriel, excuse me," Blixen said. "Do you mean to say that no one ever told you—in nine months—whether this job was permanent or not?"

"Well—no," said Miss Firebush.

"You're joking."

"No."

Blixen slumped back in his chair. "Well, it is."

"Oh." Miss Firebush ran a finger under the rubber band around the dictation book and broke it, then bent over to blindly search for it.

"What a fantastic situation," Blixen said.

"Mr. Blixen," Miss Firebush said toward the carpet, "please don't blame the head of the secretarial pool. I mean, she's been busy."

"I *don't* blame her," Blixen said. "I blame myself."

"Oh. Well . . ."

"Do you know what male chauvinism is, Muriel?"

"Uh, not really."

"Male chauvinism," Blixen said, "is the unique ability a man has to come into an office day after day, to expect to be waited on hand and foot by a warm, sympathetic woman, to load her with work too dull for his own swift mind, to pay her less than she's worth, to kill her ambition and never, under any circumstances at all, to see her as a human being with fears and rights of her own. *That* is male chauvinism, and I've been as guilty of it as Archie Bunker and it makes me want to vomit. I apologize with all my heart."

Miss Firebush, still searching for the broken rubber band, nodded sharply and wordlessly.

"And to cap everything," Blixen said, "I haven't even had the courtesy to ask if *you* want the job."

"Oh," Miss Firebush said in a hoarse honk. "Okay."

"Let the rubber band go," Blixen said. "The cleaner'll find it to-night."

Miss Firebush nodded again, shot to her feet, and never looked back as she fled.

Dazed, Blixen took his coffee to the window and stood looking out at the long afternoon shadows and thought about facades and the status quo and how ruinously difficult it was to change a comfortable point of view. The coffee, for instance. There was no law of business that required secretaries to become housekeeper-waitresses as well. And yet how comfortable it was that they were, and how difficult it would be for executives to relinquish even this small perquisite. To be served—to be given the proper amount of cream or sugar, or sugar substitute, instead of strychnine, or . . .

Outside, a butterfly staggered past his window like a blown scrap of paper, but he scarcely noticed it. He felt a tingling in his hand; when he looked down he saw that he'd spilled his coffee somehow. Stupidly he put the cup back on his desk and wiped his hand with his handkerchief, thinking again, forcing himself to think again: *coffee—sugar substitute—bitter—strychnine . . .* ? And then: *my God—yes—yes— that's how it was done—and that's who the target was . . .*

He rubbed a throbbing vein over his left eye for a time, suddenly aware of how fast the room was cooling, of how cold his flesh was, and then he swung back to his desk and picked up his phone. He pressed the intercom button.

Miss Firebush, in tears, managed a strangled, "Yes . . ." and in a voice he barely recognized he told her that he'd like to speak to David Sanderson, who probably could be reached at the Cucaracha Restaurant in Oceanport. "Sandstrom," Miss Firebush said wetly, "Coucharia Restaurant," and rang off.

But he knew the miracle would repeat itself and that she would certainly succeed in contacting his party even under those mangled names and even if he'd misdirected her and Sanderson turned out to be in China rather than Oceanport. He expected all this quite automatically, the way a farmer expects spring, and when she buzzed him back, he pressed the lighted flashing button on line two and said: "Hello, David, this is Nils."

"Hi, Nils."

"Hi."

"What's up?"

"How's everything?"

"Here? Couldn't be calmer."

"David—couple of questions . . ."

"Shoot."

Blixen cradled the phone between his shoulder and neck and hefted one of the heavy-headed hippos. He cleared his throat. "Tell me—is Isabel around?"

"Isabel? No. Why?"

"Of course you do know where she is?"

"Well, I suppose she's down by the beach. She went for a walk. I didn't want her to, but you've been witness to the remarkable influence I have over this woman. One word from me and she does as she pleases."

"Is she alone?"

"She was when she left."

"Why didn't you go with her, David? I asked you to keep an eye on her."

"She wouldn't hear of it. . . . Nils? What's wrong?"

The hippo in Blixen's hand had been designed with its head back, roaring. But gripped like this, held on the perpendicular, its effort looked less like a roar than a scream. "A good deal, I'm afraid," Blixen said. "I think somebody's out to kill her."

There was a vacant pause on the line. "You think what?" Sanderson asked.

The throbbing vein was back; Blixen jammed his thumb against it. "Does she still use the same type of sugar substitute? The crystalline kind?"

"The—? What's sugar substitute got to do—"

"Does she still take as much as she did?"

"If the coffee needs it, she pours it in. But, Nils, listen—"

"So she tries the coffee first?"

"Always."

"Then," Blixen said wearily, "that's it. That has to be it. There's no other explanation."

"What's—"

"She told me last night that there couldn't have been strychnine in the coffee, David, because she'd had some herself, and it hadn't hurt her. But that's where the dog *must* have gotten it. In the coffee. He hadn't eaten anything else. Which means that Isabel tried it first— then put the sweetener in—and then gave it to Harpo without tasting it again."

"Oh, my God . . ."

"How does she carry it?"

"In a bottle—little square—"

"Where's the bottle now?"

"Now," Sanderson said, and stopped; Blixen could hear him breathing deeply and regularly. "Well," he said at last, "it must still be in her bag. I saw it there this afternoon."

"When?"

"We had breakfast at about one o'clock in a coffee shop on Leavenworth. I bought her a pack of cigarettes and I saw the bottle when she put the cigarettes in her purse."

"Are you saying it was never *out* of the purse?"

"I'm—I think I'm saying that."

"Did either of you order coffee?"

"Did either of us order coffee?" Sanderson repeated like a quiz-show contestant facing the clock, facing disaster. "Yes. No. No, I didn't want any, so Isabel decided she'd skip it, too. She thinks it makes her heart race. She said she'd have some tea later on."

"And did she?"

"Yes," Sanderson said.

"When?"

"About fifteen minutes ago. Just before she left."

"Well," Blixen said, and put down the screaming hippo and rested his cheek against his knuckles, "if she used sweetener in the tea, then I think you'd better call an ambulance and round up Jesus and anybody else you can find and have them help you comb the town for that poor lady, and I think you'd better start right now."

"Do I have to tell you," Sanderson said, "that the fog has just come in so bloody thick down here you can't see your hand in front of your face?"

"Hurry."

"I'm on my way."

CHAPTER FOURTEEN

Blinded, hands dug into her pants pockets, she missed the curb and fell heavily into a black puddle. She thought that she must have cut her ankle, perhaps broken it, but when she rolled over and climbed to her feet she found that she could stand without too much pain.

"David?" she cried. And then: "*DA-VID!*"

But there was no answer. She might have been yelling on the airless moon. She had no idea where she was, where the restaurant might be, how far she had come before the fog had fallen around her like a soiled cocoon. A blurred rectangle above her head on a yellowish lamppost could have been a street sign, but her migraine was at its height now and she doubted that she could have read the sign even in the clearest sunlight.

Her likeliest guess was that she had been on the corner of C and Kaw when she'd lost her bearings. At any rate, she had fumbled her way down Kaw, toward the beach, and presently seemed to be in an alley something like the alley behind the restaurant.

Her skull shook under the hammering of the headache; her brain felt covered with paper-cuts; her stomach heaved. Keeping one hand on a slippery wall to guide her, she limped down the alley.

Oh, this is a bad one, she thought, this is a very, very bad one; this is a blind headache to make a believer out of Mary Baker Eddy. . . .

It was odd. In her family, migraines had been called 'blind headaches' since her mother's grandmother had died of one in 1868. Or reportedly had died of one. That was what the women claimed. To a man the family's men always had doubted it because blind headaches were so exclusively female, skipping the men altogether, handed down from mother to daughter like some giddy and convenient talent, fortune-telling or double-jointedness.

Even Isabel had doubted it, aligning herself as a tomboy sternly behind the men, scoffing and snorting at her mother's symptoms, *plus royaliste que le roi.*

Until a day on a bus in Waco, when she discovered that she could see only half of the scene around her.

She had presumed at first that she had offended God again and that He had decided to strike her blind. But when she had found her way home, after swearing on her sacred word to enter a nunnery the second the Holy Mother intervened on her behalf and had her vision restored, her own mother had loaded aspirins into her, put her briskly to bed in a darkened room, and told her not to be so opinionated in the future. She had the blind headache.

It had infuriated her and yet comforted her, like menstruation, as if she had somehow been officially enrolled in the league of women. She learned almost to anticipate the onset of the strange semiblindness; she decided that it probably had something to do with the liver and something to do with the emotions, perhaps equally. Overdieting and too many tests at school could bring it on. Fears for Jesus Mary could bring it on. Her defiance of Blixen had brought this one on, coupled with her inability to make David understand her position.

Stumbling, she brushed against a peeling poster on a filthy brick wall, scratching her hand and doing God alone knew what to the coat she was wearing. She would never be able to explain the coat. She had grabbed up the first thing she had come across at the restaurant doorway, which had happened to be Enid Billroth's white wool, and had taken Enid's white umbrella too because it really had looked more like rain than fog when she had set out, and now there would be no way for her to apologize for the damage she'd done to them. . . .

A footstep scraped on the pavement behind her.

She wheeled, squinting. "David?"

The fog swirled. She was almost sure there was a form in it.

"Excuse me," she said, "but I'm afraid I'm lost. Could you—"

She faltered. Surely if there'd been someone there, he'd have spoken. "I'm sorry," she muttered, really to herself, and continued on her groping way.

Why hadn't she let David accompany her!

Well, she knew the answer to that. She hated to fight with David. But there were times when she needed to be alone even more than she needed love, certainly more than she needed lecturing. When she thought about it, there was only one person she never tired of being with, and that was Jesus Mary. As a child, she had often pretended that Jesus Mary was her real father. She had not exactly *disliked* her real father; he had been too vague, too weak to dislike. She could never remember him picking her up, holding her, playing with her. Jesus Mary had been the one to do that—the tall, strong male in her life, the image of stability and power. Maybe Jesus Mary *was* her father. He seemed to think more of her than he did of Gloria; he always had.

She was trying to imagine Jesus Mary and her mother together, trying to pick out a resemblance between Jesus Mary and herself, when she stubbed her toe on a raised back step and saw, on the brick wall nearly under her nose, the words: SALTAIRE APTS.

She couldn't help it. She was not a crier, but she burst into tears at that point and pressed a kiss onto the bricks and mumbled, "David, David, by God, I'm *home*."

And so she was. The next building down was Junkin's hardware, and the restaurant was next to that, and all she had to do now was slip into this back entrance and make her way to Enid's apartment and knock and let Gloria take care of her.

Just as soon as she could find the knob. And the strength to turn it.

Through the pounding in her head, she actually thought she heard horns—or sirens—something. And way off in the distance, David's voice . . . "Babe! Babe!"

She straightened. "David?"

Then there was a rush of footsteps behind her and she turned to anticipate him and all she saw, the last she saw, was the brittle gleam of the crowbar as it swung down toward her head.

CHAPTER FIFTEEN

"How is she?" Blixen whispered.

"Her head aches, for Christ's sake, that's how she is," Isabel snarled. " 'How is she?' 'How is she?' Jesus."

"Back to her old sweet, girlish self," Sanderson said, "as you can see."

"Darling?" Isabel said.

"Yes, babe."

"Screw off."

"One thing I'll give her in spades," Sanderson said. "She does fight the cliché. When we found her out there in the alley—"

"Wait a minute," DeGroot said from the shadows. "Who's 'we'?"

Jesus Mary, who was seated on the bed with Dr. Trout, scowling down at Isabel's white face and bandaged head and pressing her free hand roughly, said: "Me and David. He saw her first—he yelled—I came in from the other end of the alley."

"The north end?"

"I don't know. North. Yes."

"Anybody run out past you that way?"

"No."

"Past you, Sanderson?"

"No."

"What about you, Miss Chavez. Could you recognize anything at all about your assailant?"

"I *told* you, I had the blind headache! I wouldn't have recognized Milton Berle in drag."

"Mr. Sanderson, about what time—"

"Excuse me, Sheriff," Dr. Trout interrupted, "but I told you something before, too, and that was that this young lady has to rest. She isn't concussed but she's had a bad blow, a bad scare. If you must ask questions, I'd be obliged if you'd ask them somewhere else." He twisted around to glance meaningfully toward the woman in the bedroom doorway. "Why don't you fix these gentlemen some sand-wiches, Enid—in the kitchen."

"Kitchen," Mrs. Billroth replied. "Certainly. Well, you heard him. Everybody out. Doctor's orders." If she'd had an apron, Blixen thought, she'd have flapped it.

"Madam," DeGroot began.

"Sir," Mrs. Billroth cut in, "this is my apartment you're in, you're in it on my sufferance, you haven't got a warrant, you're not well liked in this neighborhood, so if I were you, I really would cool it and do as I was told. May I give you a little homely advice? Never lock a gift horse in the house."

Confused, DeGroot said: "Isn't that 'mouth'?"

"Never lock a gift horse in the mouth? Don't be ridiculous."

Jesus Mary bent forward to kiss his niece on the tip of the nose. "Good night, heart," he growled in Spanish. "Sleep well."

"Good night, tio."

"I'll see you tomorrow, babe," Sanderson said.

"Yes . . ."

Following Blixen out the doorway, DeGroot grunted: "What the hell is it?"

"Never *sock* a gift horse in the mouth," Blixen said.

"No, it isn't," DeGroot said, "it's 'look, look.' If you goddamn bleeding-heart liberals knew what a pain in the ass you were when you clowned around like that, you wouldn't do it." Red-necked, he clumped off after Jesus Mary into the kitchen.

Sanderson had turned the other way, into the miniscule sitting room, so Blixen closed the bedroom door gently on Trout and Isabel and headed in that direction, too.

He found his story editor standing beside a side window, peering dully at an ancient geranium in a broken pot on the outside sill. The room was shabby, cluttered with knickknacks from the years before the war. There was a folding Japanese screen discreetly hiding a false fireplace. Plaster Chinese heads hung like trophies on the walls. Gloria lay on a herniated sofa, wrapped in a shawl, toasting her shoe-less feet at a portable gas heater that was tied to its wall jet by a limp green hose.

"That's illegal, you know," Blixen said.

Gloria lifted her head. "What is?"

"Unvented heater."

"Oh." She let her head drop again. "So are the termites in the building. So are the blocked fire escapes. Go argue with the absentee owners." Perturbed, she slid the garnet ring on her right hand back and forth, back and forth.

"Pretty stone," Blixen said.

The hand vanished under the shawl. For a second Gloria's eyes remained tightly closed. Then she sat up, fishing under the couch for her shoes. "Excuse me," she said.

Sanderson, puzzled, watched her go, then glanced at Blixen. "Strange effect you have on that girl," he said.

"Perhaps it was a clumsy compliment."

"Why should it have been?"

"I have no idea."

Sanderson thought about that, then shrugged and flopped onto the couch in Gloria's place. "God, what a day," he said.

"So," Blixen said. "Tell me about it."

"Starting where? You probably know as much as I do. She hadn't ingested any strychnine—"

"Are they positive?"

"The doctors on the ambulance seemed to be. I kept screaming, 'Pump her stomach, pump her stomach!' until they must have wanted to pump *mine,* just to shut me up. But there really wasn't any indication of poisoning, no symptoms whatsoever. She complained of nausea, but that was absolutely consistent with these blind headaches she gets. And then when I found the bottle in her purse, and it turned out that there wasn't any strychnine in that either—"

"Hold it," Blixen said.

"I know," Sanderson said, "it's the only way the dog could have been poisoned. I can't help it. They tested the thing right in front of my eyes. No strychnine."

"Same bottle? Same sugar substitute?"

"Same everything."

Blixen crossed to the alley window and stood facing his own reflection blankly. "Then that's worse," he said.

"Worse? How?"

"Because it means that the poisoner's someone very close to her, doesn't it." Blixen turned to him. "Close enough to have poisoned the bottle to begin with, and to have replaced the original sweetener when the trick backfired."

"But that has to include everybody at the restaurant," Sanderson protested. "Gloria, Judy, Jesus Mary, Mrs. Billroth, me—"

"And a couple of others."

"Nils," Sanderson said, "couldn't it be a simple—"

"How does Isabel explain the attack tonight?"

"She thinks it was a mugging. Attempted mugging."

"Somebody after her bag?"

"Yes."

"Did they try to grab it?"

"I don't believe there was time," Sanderson said. "I must have practically run into the guy. I heard him drop his crowbar."

"He used a *crowbar?*"

"Small crowbar. Evidently he'd found it in the alley. It was one of Junkin's."

"All right, you heard him drop the crowbar," Blixen said, "but you didn't hear him run off?"

"Well, I heard *running,*" Sanderson said, "but it turned out to be Jesus Mary."

"I suppose he could have slipped by one of you in the fog."

"Might have—or he might have jumped into the apartment house. That back hall runs straight through to the front. The only trouble with that is that Gloria came roaring out of Mrs. Billroth's place the minute she heard Isabel scream, and she didn't see anybody in the hall."

"About how big would you estimate this crowbar was, David?"

"Oh—" Sanderson measured an imaginary trout between his hands.

"So a woman could have lifted it—swung it—"

"Sure. Easily."

"I wonder why it did so little damage, though," Blixen said.

"How do you mean?"

"Well, you'd think even a child could have put enough weight behind a blow like that to fracture a skull."

"Isabel caught it on her umbrella," Sanderson said. "She lifted her umbrella—I guess automatically—and the crowbar hit the umbrella and the *umbrella* hit her."

"I didn't know Isabel owned an umbrella."

"She doesn't. It's Enid's. Mrs. Billroth's."

"Mrs. *Bill*roth's?"

Sanderson grinned. "That's what I was going to say when DeGroot butted in back in the bedroom. That kid doesn't have a clichéd bone in her body. Here she was in this classic setup, flat on her behind, coming to with Jesus Mary and me bending over her . . . what should she have said? What would Joan *Crawford* have said?"

" 'Where—am I?' "

"Not our babe." Sanderson beamed. "Our babe says—"

"Leaving out the obscenities."

"Leaving out the obscenities, yes—our *babe* says, 'Hey, look what that mother-lover did to Enid's best umbrella!' " Chuckling, Sanderson added: "I told her, I said, 'Damn it, sweetheart, you're going to have to stay away from Enid's property before you strip her naked.' The umbrella, the coat . . ."

Blixen, pacing by the window, stopped. "The coat? What coat?"

"Well, she was also wearing Enid's white coat. That was a mess. She'd already torn it once."

Slowly Blixen walked back to the sofa. "When?"

"The first night she was here. I told you about that. The car that almost hit her?"

"And she was wearing—"

"Enid's coat, right, both times." Sanderson's voice trailed off. He sat up. "Nils."

"Enid's coat," Blixen said, "Enid's umbrella . . . going into Enid's apartment. They're both about the same height, same general build—"

"Hoo-hoo," Mrs. Billroth rasped from the hallway, "who wants coffee in here? Anybody?" She carried a steaming pot in one hand; Gloria lurked behind her with a tray of cups. "I'm out of sugar," Mrs. Billroth apologized. "I forget to buy it. Can you stand artificial sweetener? The crystals? I guess Isabel and me are the only ones in this neck of the forest who ever use it."

She peered uncertainly at their faces. "Plenty of cream, though," she said.

CHAPTER SIXTEEN

"Just plain black for me," Dr. Trout boomed.

For a while Mrs. Billroth continued to stand like a statue, her back to the wall and Trout, her eyes fixed on Blixen through the coffeepot steam. "Well," she said at last, "I didn't have an accident, but I'll never know why." She took a breath. "Hello, Harold," she said.

"Hi, there," Trout said.

"Harold," said Mrs. Billroth, "I'm going to be candid with you. If you ever—if you *ever* come creeping up on me like that again, I'll turn around, and I'll take hold of the first limb on your body I come to, and I'll break it off."

"Oh?" Trout said. "Well, I didn't scare Gloria. Did I, dear?"

"You sure as hell did," Gloria said. "I'm still trembling."

Trout's mournful bloodhound eyes, over the bifocals, swept the room. "You all must have had your minds on something indecent then. I didn't clump, but I certainly—"

"Doctor, excuse me." Blixen came forward. "Mrs. Billroth, could I ask you a question?"

"If you'll wait for my heart to stop pounding."

"Say when."

"Oh, when, when. Go ahead. I don't care."

"*Why* do you forget to buy sugar?"

"She can't take it," Trout put in. "She's diabetic."

"Adult diabetes," Mrs. Billroth said. "I'm on the pills, not insulin. I just have to be careful."

Blixen glanced at Dr. Trout. "And—I suppose all this is generally known around here?"

Trout seemed surprised. "Well, I presume so."

"As a matter of fact," said Mrs. Billroth, "that was my sugar-substitute bottle those men from the ambulance were testing. I kept telling them there was no strychnine in it. I couldn't believe my ears. How could there be strychnine in it?"

"How did Isabel get your bottle, Mrs. Billroth?" Blixen asked.

"She ran out, so she wondered if she could borrow some from me. I had a bottle in the cupboard. I told her to take that."

"And when did all this happen?"

"Monday."

"How long had it been since you had used the crystals?"

"Personally? Well, let me see. About a week."

"A week . . ."

Confused, Mrs. Billroth said: "I really don't see what this is leading to. I mean, the ambulance men said there wasn't any poison in the bottle. And Isabel wasn't poisoned anyway. She was struck on the head."

"How *is* the big star, by the way?" Gloria asked.

"She's sleeping," Trout replied. "She'll be up and around tomorrow."

"I must say, Doctor," Blixen put in, "I think I would have felt easier in my own mind if you'd sent her on to a hospital—for observation."

"So would I," Trout agreed. "But she wouldn't go. Flatly refused."

"She told us," Sanderson said, "that she'd tear the place apart if we hospitalized her. And when Isabel threatens, wise men listen."

"Yeah, that's one thing about Miss Mexico," Gloria remarked. "She means what she says."

"Gloria," Trout said, "you put the wrong interpretation on that scene. Isabel was rambling, she was barely conscious."

"You shouldn't be so sensitive, missy," said Mrs. Billroth. "I never knew you were like that."

"There's a lot people don't know about me," Gloria said. "I'm a real enigma." She caught Blixen's gaze on her right hand; abruptly she jerked off the ring and dropped it into her skirt pocket. "I have to find my *novio*."

"I'd like someone to stay with Isabel for a few minutes while I look in on Judith," Trout said.

Gloria turned. "Well, I can't."

"Gloria!" Mrs. Billroth called, hurrying after her. "Gloria!"

Trout fetched a sigh up from his boots. "So much for the coffee," he said.

"I'll do that, by the way," Sanderson said.

"Do what?"

"Stay with Isabel."

"Oh—would you? I shouldn't be more than a few minutes."

"Care if I tag along, Doctor?" Blixen asked.

The old brown face lit up. "With me? Oh, I'd like that very much." He gestured toward the door. "Please."

They dropped off Sanderson at the bedroom and strolled on toward the rear of the apartment house. There was no sign of DeGroot or Jesus Mary; in the kitchen Gloria was weeping uncontrollably in Mrs. Billroth's arms. Mrs. Billroth raised her eyes to heaven when they looked in, and patted Gloria on the shoulder.

In the back entry, Trout pointed up the rickety stairs and said: "That's my place, by the way, at the top of the landing. I know you're worried about Miss Chavez, but I can assure you she's perfectly all right. And even if she should need another sleeping pill, or reassurance, or anything like that, I'm less than a minute away."

"I'm not worried, Doctor. If you say she's medically sound, then she's medically sound."

"She's medically sound," Trout said. A sob reached their ears and he glanced significantly back at the kitchen. *"There's* the girl who's apt to need attention tonight," he said.

"She *is* an enigma, isn't she."

"Like all of us."

He opened the rear door and Blixen stepped outside. The fog had begun to lift, although it was still impossible to see the stars. In the channel, a ship's horn blew gutturally.

"What happened between them tonight?" Blixen asked.

"Between—?"

"Between Gloria and Isabel."

Trout puffed out his cheeks, stumbled, and grabbed Blixen's arm. "Oh, it was ridiculous, the whole business," he said. "Silly. Isabel was in shock, rambling on about the last thing, probably, that had been in her head when she was hit, and Gloria took offense at it. Absurd. I told her so at the time."

"Is it a private matter, or . . . ?"

"I can't think why it should be. Isabel was speculating as to whether or not Jesus Mary might be her real father. She said in a very childish manner that she'd always felt that he loved her more than he did Gloria. Well, this hurt Gloria."

"I can see where it might."

"Um? Well—yes . . ."

"I can't find much resemblance, Doctor, between Gloria and Jesus Mary—can you?"

"Takes after her mother," Trout said. "Have you met the mother?"

"Not yet."

"Takes very much after the mother. You'll see . . . Watch your step here. Junkin wasn't the neatest shopkeeper on earth."

Behind the hardware store the alley was strewn with rusted parts. Blixen stepped over a two-wheeled tiltback dolly and squinted through the dark rear window into what appeared to be Junkin's office. " 'Wasn't'?" he murmured. "You think he's dead, then, do you?"

"I don't know. I wish I'd seen that butchered body," Trout answered. "DeGroot certainly thinks so. He's been after me and after me to visit the morgue. I told him I'd be in tomorrow afternoon. They can't lure the wife down."

"Will you be able to make a positive identification?"

"One way or the other. I've asked them to take X rays. I'll compare those with mine of Junkin."

Wiping his hands, Blixen eased away from the window. "I'd like you to call me when you do come to a decision," he said. "One way or the other. I'm very interested in this."

"Yes, all right."

They continued on toward the restaurant. "Speaking of disappearances," Blixen mused, "I don't believe I've seen Cabral around tonight."

"Come to think of it, neither have I," Trout said. "I know he's been talking about getting a job lately. He may have shipped out on one of the fishing boats."

"Is that his profession? Fisherman?"

Trout shook his head. "He's been on strike. He cuts meat. He's a butcher." Startled by his own words, Trout stopped dead.

Blixen walked on a pace or two, then paused and looked back.

"Of course it needn't *mean* anything," Trout said.

"Of course not."

"I'm sure it doesn't," Trout muttered.

"Cabral isn't too fond of Mrs. Billroth, is he?"

"Isn't he? I have no idea. Well . . . perhaps not."

"Or does he call everyone Mrs. Bitch?"

Trout's eyes glittered. "Is that what he called Enid?"

"That's one of the things he called her."

"Damned pup."

"Why don't they get along, Doctor?"

"She gets along with him, *he's* the one who—" Trout clamped his mouth shut, made an angry stab with his hand. "It's an old story, old story, tired old story . . ."

"I'd like to hear it."

"In God's name, why?"

"Why not?"

Trout examined him closely, then snatched off his glasses and wiped them on his sleeve. "All right, why not?" He stuck the glasses, more smudged than before, across his nose again and plunged his hands into his pockets. "Well, it goes all the way back to the 1950s —'54, '55."

"Cabral couldn't have been very old."

"Eight or nine. I remember what a disagreeable boy he was— egotistical, overweight, whiny. His father was a Portuguese gardener who'd come out from Colorado during the war, when the Japanese were relocated. You may not recall that shameful episode . . ."

"I recall it," Blixen said.

"At any rate, the Cabrals were convinced they had a genius on their hands. Another Heifetz. Their fat little son was a violinist."

"Good?"

"Beautiful technique. He'd been playing since he was four. He'd had the best teachers wherever he'd gone. They wanted him to have the best teacher in Oceanport. So when they moved here, they took him to Larry Billroth."

"Enid's—?"

"Husband."

"I wondered if there was a Mr. Billroth."

"You bet there was," Trout said. "I never knew a man I liked more. I never heard a better fiddler." He brushed at the remaining wisps of fog. "Anyway, they took him to Larry. And Larry told him to play anything he wanted. So the boy went through the Paganini Caprices. Do you know the Caprices?"

"No."

"They're not for amateurs, let me assure you. Cabral made a couple of little mistakes, nothing important, and Larry asked to hear the Adagio of the Brahms G Major sonata—and—that was enough—he knew what was wrong."

Blixen looked over, waiting.

"This consummate technician," Trout said, "this new Heifetz, was tone-deaf."

After a moment Blixen said: "Excuse me—I'm not a musician, but how could—"

"Why hadn't someone spotted it before? They must have. But how do you tell parents like that and a performer like that to forget about a career they'd all been preparing years for? And then, too, he wasn't always off. His fingers usually found the right notes automatically. But he couldn't count on that. His ear couldn't compensate for the slips any performer is bound to make."

"Easier just to go on teaching him, I suppose . . ."

"It wouldn't have been easier for Larry. On the other hand, he couldn't bear to tell the boy himself. So Enid had to do that."

They stood shoulder to shoulder, listening to the sad fog horns bray on the sea.

" 'Mrs. Bitch,' " Blixen said.

"I'm afraid it's a sore that's never going to heal," Trout said. "Naturally he felt the same way toward Larry."

"Larry's dead now?"

"Larry died about two months after that. I was never so shocked in my life. He was a young man, just thirty."

"What happened?"

"Heart."

"At *thirty?*"

"I know what you're thinking," Trout said. "I wondered about it, too. But if Cabral had anything to do with that death, he must have been a voodoo priest. Enid insisted on an autopsy. It turned out that Larry had had the arteries of a man twice his age. He'd been living on borrowed time for years."

Reflectively Blixen started away toward the restaurant.

Pacing beside him, Trout said: "It's the fact that Cabral's a butcher, I think, that's focused our eyes in his direction. And, really, that's quite unfair. I mean, a man might learn to use a knife in any of a hundred trades." He held up his own hands. "Like surgery. Or hadn't you thought of that?"

"Oh, I'd thought of it, Doctor," Blixen said. "I'd thought of it."

CHAPTER SEVENTEEN

They were stopped halfway up the restaurant's back stairs by one of DeGroot's deputies, a nervous youngster who bustled through the kitchen to shine his light in their faces and ask them for identification in the self-conscious yap of a battle-zone sentry. Trout said he was Dr. Trout, for God's sake, that he had been up and down these same stairs half a dozen times today, and that on four of those occasions he had been asked that same stupid question in that same rude tone and he was getting pretty sick of it. The gentleman with him, he pointed out, was Mr. Nils Blixen, they were friends of the family, they were not vandals, they were not customers, they had no intention of eating anything or harming anyone, and they would deeply appreciate it if DeGroot would drop his police-state tactics and allow honest citizens to go about their normal business unmolested.

Visibly hurt, the deputy replied that he was only doing his duty, that they had already had more trouble with this assignment than it was worth and that they didn't want any more. Then he did a stiff about-face and started to march off.

But before he could get away, Blixen said: "Deputy—one thing more . . ."

Angrily the deputy hitched around.

"Were you on duty here all afternoon?" Blixen asked.

"I was, yes."

"Were you here when Miss Chavez was attacked out in the alley?"

"I was here, but I didn't know she was being attacked."

"Didn't hear her scream?"

"All I heard," said the deputy, "was a couple of men yelling that they'd found her. I rushed out onto the back porch, but I couldn't see anything through the fog."

"Was anybody else here?"

"The woman upstairs was in bed, I guess, and the other woman—

Mrs. Billroth—she ran downstairs to ask me what all the hollering was, and then she took off."

"The lower floor was empty at the time—except for you?"

"Yes."

"Thank you."

The deputy glared at Trout and tramped back through the kitchen, banging chairs out of the way and slamming doors.

"He wanted me to apologize," Trout said, "but I'd be damned if I would. He started it."

"Well, this business has made us all edgy," Blixen said.

"I'll apologize when I'm wrong, but not when I'm right." Grumbling under his breath, Trout led the way up the stairs to a low hall, then indicated a closed doorway. "In here." He rapped twice.

"Si, quien?" a woman called in a querulous, weak voice.

"Are you decent?" Trout asked.

"Who is it?"

"Cary Grant."

"Sure," the woman said, "I *would* be decent when Cary Grant drops by. Come on in."

Trout opened the door; over the doctor's shoulder Blixen could see a blond woman with long, loose hair and pain-ravaged, horselike features sitting up in a rumpled twin bed, smoothing the covers over her knees. A stout blackthorn cane stood within reach of her hand.

She smiled at Trout. "Gulled again," she said. "You're no more Cary Grant than I am."

"No, I'm not," Trout confessed. "I lied."

"Story of my life."

"Men lie a lot to you, do they?"

"Over and over."

Trout moved further into the room and the blond woman caught sight of Blixen.

"Don't worry," Trout said, "he's just a friend." To Blixen, he explained: "I offered to bring a psychiatrist around one day to see if *he* could help that back of hers, and she's felt threatened ever since."

"I don't either feel threatened. I just don't believe in that mumbo-jumbo."

"Brouwer believes in it," Trout said. "*I* believe in it."

"Fine. You believe what you want, I'll believe what I want."

Sighing, Trout said: "Judy Chavez—may I present Mr. Nils Blixen."

"Well!" Judy said. "Hi there. So you're him."

"I'm him," Blixen said. "Hi."

"I sure never thought I'd—" She stopped short; her face clouded. "Doctor," she said, "everything's copacetic, isn't it? You two didn't come over here to tell me something?"

"What? Tell you what?"

"Is Isabel all right?"

Trout snorted. "I assured you she was all right twenty minutes after I bandaged her head. Didn't you believe me?"

"You also assured me you were Cary Grant."

"Bandaged heads I don't fool around about." Trout studied her compassionately and then smiled. "No, she's resting easily. I just wanted to see how you were doing after all the excitement, and Mr. Blixen here asked if he could come along."

"Is Enid with Isabel?"

"Enid's with her, but Enid said she'd be back here before you fell asleep tonight."

"I don't think she'll have to hurry. I'm about as sleepy as a fire alarm."

"Is your back worse?"

"Killing me."

"Take another sedative when Enid gets here."

"I don't want to depend on drugs. What's the point? I want to walk!" She grimaced at Blixen. "Isn't this the limit? Flat on my back just when everybody needs me the most."

"You'll be up again as soon as the muscles stop spasming," Blixen said.

"Yeah, I know."

"How about those exercises I gave you?" Trout interjected. "They help any?"

"They hurt my legs."

"Still the same tenderness in your lower spine?"

"It's worse."

"Roll over."

"Well—now . . . ?"

"Eh?"

"I'll wait outside," Blixen said.

"Oh! All right, suit yourself. Or you can just turn your back if you want." To Judy, Trout added: "If he starts twitching and swooping at you, I'll trip him and you hit him with the cane."

"We don't want to kill him, we'll just stun him," Judy said.

"Exactly."

Turning, Blixen said: "I won't even breathe hard."

"Well, that you can do," Judy told him. The bed creaked. "Been a while since anybody breathed very hard about me."

"This hurt?" Trout murmured.

"Um! Yes."

"Here?"

"Yes!"

There was a posed studio photograph of Gloria on a shelf above an ornate, opened family Bible. Blixen bent close to it. No rings.

"That's my daughter," Judy mumbled.

"Yes, I've met her. Charming young woman."

"Gloria's okay."

"I was admiring a ring of hers. I notice she isn't wearing it here."

"Ring? Oh. That. Isn't she?"

"Well, there's nothing out of place," Trout grunted. "You could have some spinal arthritis."

"Great."

The Bible had been opened to the Psalms. Blixen flipped through to the back, glanced down the list of names and dates written in faded ink under Family Chronicle. The last birth entry was: GLORIA RAFAELA CHAVEZ, 1/29/49.

"Where'd she get that ring?" Blixen asked. "Do you remember?"

"No, I don't," Judy said.

"The garnet?" Trout's voice was surprised. "Why, you do, too. It was in that mysterious package that came for Gloria from Mexico a couple of months ago. End of January. From Mazatlan."

"Oh, was it? I don't recall."

"End of January," Blixen repeated. "By the way, what's the birth-stone for January?"

"No idea in the world," Judy said.

"Isn't it the garnet?" Trout inquired.

"Garnet," Blixen said. "Yes, I think it is."

CHAPTER EIGHTEEN

By the time Mrs. Billroth arrived to relieve them it was ten minutes to nine and Dr. Trout, who had promised to walk Blixen over to Brouwer's church on the southern edge of the city, said he was sorry but that he was afraid he just wasn't going to be able to make it. He said he'd been up since six, running around like a chicken with its head cut off, and about all he had the strength left to do was look in once more on Isabel and then go to bed himself.

So Blixen wished him good night in front of the restaurant, and set off, alone, southward down A.

The fog had left the streets wet and deserted. Now and again a dog would lunge hysterically at him from behind the safety of a rugged fence, but there was no sign whatsoever of people in the meager yards or behind the dirty curtains in the lonely lighted windows. No one bothered him in this bigoted enclave, no one greeted him. Murder had been done up the street, and by now the doors were as locked as the minds.

Brouwer's church turned out to be a narrow white wooden building in need of paint and a taller steeple. It was perched on the edge of an estuary that stood as one of the city's boundary lines. A high, flimsy wooden bridge spanned the neck of the estuary here, and Brouwer leaned against the rail midway across it, spitting into the blackness below. He gave a spasmodic start when Blixen hailed him. "Yes!" he cried. "Who's there? Who is that?"

"I'm sorry, Reverend," Blixen called. "I didn't realize how dark it was here on the bank. It's Nils Blixen." He walked onto the bridge. "Sorry."

"Well, for Pete's sake," Brouwer said. "You're back."

"Yes."

"I'm glad. I'm surprised, but I'm glad."

"Surprised why?"

Dispiritedly Brouwer pushed his coonskin cap forward and leaned again on the rail. "Oh, I don't know. I suppose it's because I always expect everyone else to react the way I do. One look inside that barrel and I was ready to cut out of Oceanport forever. Bigots I can handle. Butchers are something else."

"Yet you're still here."

"Um. Well, if that's a virtue, it's a negative one. The fight's between cowardice and greed. I don't want to give up my job."

Blixen rested his forearms on the rail beside the younger man. "So what did you do today then? Just stick around here?"

"I worked, scrubbed the whole place down, kept myself worn out."

"Where were you at four-thirty—when the fog rolled in?"

"Scrubbing." Brouwer wrinkled his forehead. "Why? What happened at four-thirty?"

"There was another incident," Blixen said. "Up by the restaurant."

Brouwer straightened. "Another—!"

"Isabel Chavez was attacked."

Staring, Brouwer whispered: "Isabel! What is this, the end of the world? Has everybody gone crazy? Have they—" He broke off, squeezing his hands together. "Poor thing, poor little thing . . . Was she badly hurt?"

"Just shaken up."

"I hope they caught whoever did it."

"Unfortunately he got away."

"It was a man then."

"No one knows."

"I understood you to—"

"Whoever did it," Blixen said, "got away."

"I see. Well—if DeGroot wants to interview any of my congregation, he can come to the prayer meeting tomorrow night. They'll all be here—all God's superpatriots."

"You think one of your congregation might be behind this?"

Brouwer moved his shoulders uneasily. "I've—sensed a very black mood developing down here since Junkin's disappearance, Mr. Blixen. Cabral and I were talking about it only this afternoon—"

"Cabral?" Blixen interrupted. "Cabral was *here* this afternoon? With you?"

"That's right. He came by about four."

"And when did he leave?"

"Well—whenever the fog lifted . . . He was here for several hours." Brouwer's round face grew baffled. "Is it important?"

"I don't know," Blixen said. The dark sea water below them sucked and slapped at its banks. At last Blixen shook his head. "I'm sorry. You were saying something about a black mood . . ."

"Well, yes," Brouwer said. "Almost everyone I talk to seems to think that Junkin's dead, and that Jesus Mary shot him. They don't reason it out, they don't *want* to reason it out. They just want to punish somebody."

"What's the general attitude toward Enid Billroth?"

"Toward *Enid?* Everybody loves Enid."

"And yet," Blixen reminded him, "Enid was the one who started the ball rolling in the first place. By selling to Chavez."

"Yes," Brouwer said stubbornly, "but that wouldn't matter, everybody loves Enid. I can't think of a single soul who doesn't consider that woman the salt of the earth."

Blixen glanced at his set profile and then returned his gaze to the water. "Have you ever heard Ray Cabral play the violin?"

"Yes, I have," Brouwer answered. "And he's marvelous. He could be a professional." He hesitated. "Now there's a job he could handle . . ."

"Musician?"

"Violinist. I know he's been worried about money. He asked to borrow some from me this afternoon. I wonder why he hasn't tried to find work in one of the clubs around here . . . I'll suggest it to him when he gets back."

Blixen broke a splinter from the rail, stuck it in his mouth, and then very casually turned his head to Brouwer. "Where's he gone?"

"Who, Cabral?" Brouwer chuckled. "You'll never believe it."

"Try me."

"He's grunion hunting. He'd be at it right now, as a matter of fact."

Blixen chewed meditatively on his splinter.

Brouwer pointed up at the sky. "Full moon. He's heard they're running on one of the beaches south of here."

"Are they, indeed?"

Brouwer examined him. "You don't believe in grunion, do you."

"Maybe it's because I've never seen one."

"Have you ever seen Afghanistan?"

Blixen smiled. "All right, Reverend, tell me about grunion."

"Well, they're small, like smelt. They spawn on the beaches anywhere from Baja to Santa Barbara starting about this time of year."

"During the full moon."

"Full or new moon. They come as far up the beach as the highest tide'll take 'em—lay and fertilize their eggs—and then two weeks later, the next high tide washes the eggs out of the sand and hatches them."

"And exactly where is all this happening?"

"Cabral wasn't sure. Somewhere between here and Baja."

"He'd be a hard man to locate, wouldn't he," Blixen said.

"Yes, he would."

"Very convenient."

"Convenient?"

"For someone who wants to get away from it all."

"Oh," Brouwer said, "yes. Very."

In the darkness ahead of them, the surf boomed; the evening sounds along the estuary reached their ears faintly. Scurryings. A snap. Multitudinous little murders. Unexpectedly Brouwer said: "Mr. Blixen, have you ever thought of killing yourself?"

"Not too seriously."

"Cabral has. He told me so today."

"Did he tell you why?"

"No. I was—cleaning the vestry walls when he first dropped in, so I asked him to wait in the chapel. But when I finally finished, I couldn't find him. At first I thought that he'd just gone on home without saying goodbye—but that didn't seem like Cabral to me—so I went all through the church. Still couldn't find him—until I came out here."

"Onto the bridge?"

Nodding, Brouwer said: "I couldn't see him from the bank. The fog was too thick by then. But when I started across, there he was, leaning on the rail, just like this. I said, 'Why, Ray, what's wrong?' He looked very—emotional. And he said, 'Alfred, I've been standing here trying to decide whether or not I ought to jump.'" Brouwer sighed. "Well—what do you say? I came up with the usual bromides. I reminded him of all the people he'd be hurting—his parents, Gloria, his friends. I said suicide never solved anything. I said it was always darkest before the dawn. But I don't think he was even listening. He told me then that suicide wasn't a new thought to him. He said he'd considered it ever since he was nine."

"How deep is this water?" Blixen asked. "Could he have seriously hurt himself? Or was this just a verbal display for your benefit?"

"I think he could have hurt himself severely," Brouwer said. "The drop alone would stun a man, twenty-five feet. And the water's deep enough to drown in all along here. People *have* drowned in it. Of course Cabral knows how to swim. He'd instinctively try to save himself. Now, me, on the other hand—" He closed his mouth abruptly, staring down.

"You on the other hand what?" Blixen murmured. "Can't swim?"

"Not a stroke. I've always been afraid of the water. No reason for it . . ."

"Yet when I walked up here a while ago," Blixen said, "I found you leaning out over this rail like a steeplejack."

"You can be afraid of something and fascinated by it, too," Brouwer said. "Can't you . . ." He straightened. "Well." Vigorously he rubbed his hands together, thrust them under his armpits. "Getting colder. Shall we go inside?"

"What did you tell George Junkin to do when he came to you for advice, Reverend?" Blixen asked.

There was no reply. When he turned his head, Blixen saw that Brouwer had lifted his face to the moon. His eyes were shut; a pulse pounded in his throat.

"Reverend?"

"It's none of your business," Brouwer said.

"But Junkin *did* come to you?"

"I said it was none of your business."

"I wonder if you understand the problem," Blixen went on. "The fact is that DeGroot's never going to get anywhere with this case until the body in the barrel's been identified. Now, as long as he thinks it might be Junkin, he's blinding himself to—"

"It is Junkin," Brouwer said.

After a moment Blixen said: "I don't see how you can be so sure of that—unless you put him there yourself."

"I'm sure of it in my heart," Brouwer said. His eyes remained closed; a breeze flattened the coonskin fur.

"*Did* you put him there?" Blixen asked.

"No."

"Then—"

"Or maybe I did, morally." The heavy eyelids opened; haunted, Brouwer searched for something in the wide night sky. "That's the thought I can't face."

"It seems to be a thought you can't escape, either," Blixen said. "Maybe it's time you faced it."

"The difficulty is in having to face it alone," Brouwer whispered. He let his fist fall on the splintered railing. "I can't tell you how often I've wished I believed in God."

Presently Blixen said: "And I can't tell you how often your statements surprise me."

"Do they? Why?" But the words were listless. Brouwer didn't want an answer; he'd turned to face a thought. "George Junkin," he said at last, "came to see me Saturday morning. I've—never talked to a man in a worse state."

"Over what?"

"His life. His *lack* of a life. He felt that he'd never accomplished anything and now here he was middle-aged and he never would. He told me he wanted to chuck it all—his business, his wife, everything —and go to Canada. The way the kids did . . ."

"And you advised him to do that?"

Brouwer glanced over fuzzily. "To do what?"

"Chuck it all, go to Canada."

"Good Lord, no!" Brouwer exclaimed. "That's what I *should* have done! It's what any humane person would have done! I told you once that I tended to give dangerous advice. Didn't I?"

Trying to regain his balance, Blixen said: "Well, yes, but—"

"Well, what in the world could have been dangerous about going to Canada? Canada might have freed him. He might have started over." Brouwer waved an agitated hand. "No. My advice was for him to go on back to work, try to reach an accord with Jesus Mary. He said Jesus had threatened to shoot him if he so much as set foot on his property." Despairing, Brouwer looked up. "Do you know what my answer to that was?"

"I'm through with guesses," Blixen said.

"I told him to turn the other cheek!"

"Turn—"

"Are you ready for that?" Brouwer shouted. "Turn the other cheek! So of course he did! And while he was turning it, Jesus Mary shot him in the head!"

"Reverend," Blixen began.

"Oh, don't try to make excuses for me," Brouwer cried. "How do you think I felt when we found that unspeakable thing in the barrel, knowing I was an accomplice."

Blixen opened his mouth.

"Yes, I'm an accomplice!" Brouwer raved. "Certainly I'm an accomplice! Quit trying to smooth things over! I'll turn myself in! That's all I *can* do! What madman ever said confession was good for the soul?"

"Well, if not for the soul," Blixen sighed, "at least for the ego."

"For the what?" Brouwer shouted.

"Reverend," Blixen said, "Alfred—what makes you think Junkin took your advice?"

"Of course he took it!" Panting, Brouwer punched the coonskin cap further down on his head. "Naturally he took it." He tried to spit into the black water, couldn't find the saliva. "I don't know what you're getting at."

"A man comes to you," Blixen said, "wanting to have his fantasies confirmed. And what do you do?"

"I lead him astray."

"You tell him to act like a Christian instead of a child. But that isn't what he's after. He doesn't need you to point the way to righteousness. He *is* a Christian; that's the source of his agony. What he needs now is good healthy *pagan* advice."

"And for that he consults his minister?"

"For that," Blixen said, "he consults a psychiatrically oriented young man who doubts God's existence and brings rock and roll into the Sunday school."

Again Brouwer searched for saliva, raised a little this time, and spat.

"He must have thought you were crazy," Blixen said. "The last thing on earth a man like Junkin would have done is turn the other cheek to Jesus Mary."

After a time Brouwer nodded.

"He mentioned Canada, you say," Blixen mused.

"Montreal." Brouwer looked over. "Well, who *is* the man in the barrel then?"

"God knows. Someone the murderer doesn't want recognized."

"How could we recognize him from his hands?"

"Suppose they were tattooed," Blixen said. "Suppose he had a finger missing . . ."

"Yes. I see."

"Alfred—"

"Call me Al."

"Al," Blixen said, "last night you said something to me about sending people up to the restaurant. You said you wouldn't dare do that any more, even if it involved a free meal. Do you remember?"

"Yes."

"What kind of people were you talking about?"

"Well, every church gets its share of vagrants—runaway kids, people who need a place to sleep for the night and something to eat. The first time we met, Jesus Mary told me he'd be glad to feed any Mexicans who happened to drop in. So I said I'd refer them up there."

"And some did drop in, I take it."

"Well," Brouwer said, "just the one."

"One?" Blixen said.

"Now that's funny," Brouwer said. He screwed up his face, remembering. "This man already knew about the restaurant. I assumed that the word had gotten around and the Mexicans on the road were telling each other about the free meal in Oceanport." He squinted at Blixen. "But how could that be when he was the first? Nobody had *had* the free meal."

Slowly Blixen said: "What did this fellow look like, Al?"

"Short—brown hair—about fifty. I didn't pay too much attention. He wasn't here long . . ."

"When did he come in?"

"Saturday night."

"Did he say where he was from?"

"He did," Brouwer muttered. "Now where was it?"

"Educated man? How was his English?"

"Pretty good English. Not too thick an accent."

"Would you know the name of his town if you heard it?"

"I think I would."

"Was it Mazatlan?"

Brouwer snapped his fingers and pointed at Blixen. "Mazatlan!" he said. "That was it. How'd you know?"

"I can't cure myself of those wild guesses," Blixen said. He separated from Brouwer, paced to the other rail of the bridge and back again. "Did he ask about anyone special at the restaurant?"

"Like who?"

"I don't want to put words in your mouth."

"I don't think he mentioned any names."

"Didn't mention Gloria?"

"Gloria . . ." Brouwer weighed it. "No. I'm sure of that. He simply asked if the Cucaracha Restaurant was open, and off he went."

"Did you ever see him again?"

"No. But then I didn't expect to. These people never stay long in any one place."

"How did Jesus Mary react to him? Did he keep his promise? Did he give the man his free meal?"

Brouwer cocked his head. "Now that's strange. I can't remember. I don't believe he ever told me."

"Anybody up there ever mention the fellow?"

"Well, they must have . . ." Brouwer frowned at him. "Mustn't they?"

"Anything you noticed about his hands?"

"His hands . . ." Brouwer turned over his own pudgy hands as though the answer might lie somewhere there, in the folds and wrinkles along the deep lifeline. "No. I didn't see them. Maybe he kept his hands in his pockets." Brouwer filled his lungs. "Mr. Blixen," he started again shakily.

"What about his face? The shape of his head? Anything distinctive there?"

"He wore an old hat—flop-brimmed—I couldn't see his face. His hair was long in the back—brown—I remember that." Appalled, Brouwer squeezed his fingers into two fat fists. "Mr. Blixen—we couldn't possibly be right about this. Could we?"

"Somebody ended up in that barrel. For a reason. With his head and his hands cut off."

"Matthew's hand," Brouwer said heavily.

"Who's Matthew?"

"Saint Matthew. 'If thy right hand offend thee—cut it off . . .'"

After a moment, Blixen said: "And the rest of it?"

"'If thy right eye offend thee,'" Brouwer quoted, "'pluck it out, and cast it from thee: for it is profitable for thee that one of thy members should perish, and not that thy whole body should be cast into hell. . . .'"

The night sounds had quieted; even the surf seemed further away. "Thank you, Reverend," Blixen said. He studied the black swirling water below for a second or two. "There was just one other thing . . ."

"Yes?"

"You said something to me a while ago that I must have misheard.

I remember thinking that I'd have to ask you about it because it struck me as impossible."

"Oh? What was that?"

Blixen closed his eyes. "It's gone. I can't recall."

"Something about the grunion?"

"It's gone." He shook his head. "It'll come back to me. . . . Good night, Al."

"Good night, Mr. Blixen," Brouwer whispered.

CHAPTER NINETEEN

The Mexican restaurant was dark when Blixen walked by, but he saw that DeGroot's men were still on duty outside. When he lingered a little too long near the cracked front window, two uniformed deputies started toward him from across the street, and didn't stop until he called: "It's all right, officers, I'm a friend. Nils Blixen."

"They're closed, Mr. Blixen," said one of the deputies. "Everyone's asleep."

"All of them? Jesus Mary?"

"Yes, sir."

"I'll talk to him tomorrow."

"You do that."

"Good night."

"Good night, sir."

Two buildings north, the hunched gray Saltaire Apartments seemed equally dark, until Blixen groped his way down the mildewed hall to Mrs. Billroth's door, which had a slice of light under it. He rapped and was let in by Sanderson, who put a finger to his lips and murmured: "They're asleep. Where have you been?"

"With Brouwer. Who's asleep?"

"Isabel and Gloria." Sanderson tiptoed past the closed bedroom door and motioned Blixen ahead of him into the sitting room.

"I thought Gloria went to look for her *novio*," Blixen said.

Sanderson sat wearily on the sofa. "No, she telephoned a couple of places and then she gave it up."

"Where is the phone here, by the way?" Blixen asked. "I'll have to call a cab."

Sanderson pointed. "Number's on the pad there."

"David, tell me something." Blixen lifted the telephone onto his lap and dialed the number Sanderson had written down. "Did anyone at the restaurant ever mention a Mexican from Mazatlan coming by for a free meal last Saturday?"

"Mazatlan? No."

"Any Mexican visitors at all?"

"No."

"Any strangers?"

"No. What's the point, Nils? I don't understand."

So Blixen told him, while he was waiting for the cab company to answer, about his conversation with Brouwer, about the vagrant who'd asked the way to La Cucaracha and who'd kept his hands hidden, and had never been seen again.

Sanderson said: "Holy smoke," and got up to pace while the phone continued to ring monotonously in Blixen's ear. After three and a half minutes, a female dispatcher responded, interrupted him time and time again when he tried to give the address, spat at him that they might have a cab there in thirty or forty minutes, and hung up in a rage. Blixen got out his notebook, consulted it, and dialed a second number. "We'll have to run the man's disappearance down," he said. "I'll be tied up at the studio all day tomorrow. I'm flying to New York tomorrow night—"

"You are? Why?"

"One of Arthur's games. I'll be back Saturday. In the meantime—"

"Nils, if you want me back in the shop . . ."

"No, no, I want you here, with Isabel."

The phone clicked in his ear. "Hello?" Schreiber said.

"Wade? Nils."

"Yes, Nils?"

"Finally caught you at home, did I."

"Finally."

"Anything from Pep yet?"

"Well," Schreiber said, *"comme ci, comme ça.* He's not sure. He got a tentative identification on the photograph from a cab driver who thinks he might have taken Junkin to L.A. International last Saturday. But the cabbie says he dropped Junkin off at Pan American, and nobody there recognized the photo. Or the name, of course."

"Tell Pep to try Air Canada," Blixen said. "It's possible Junkin may have gone to Montreal."

"Ah, so," Schreiber said. "That *could* tie in with something Curtis Hopkins said. I talked to Curtis this afternoon—Junkin's lawyer? And Curtis told me, among other things, that Junkin had been taking French lessons off and on for the past year."

"Interesting."

"Isn't it."

"All right," Blixen said, "here's another little task for you. I want you to have someone check the court records in Bliss, Texas, to find out what was the disposition of a paternity charge filed there against Jesus Mary Chavez."

"*Bliss,* Texas?"

"Bliss."

"If you say so," Schreiber said. "What are we after?"

"It's just too complicated to spell out, Wade," Blixen said. "A crazy idea I had. If you come back with the right answer, I'll tell you."

"Isn't this fun?" Schreiber asked.

"I'll need the information as soon as possible. Before ten o'clock tomorrow night at the latest."

"Why ten o'clock?"

"I take off for New York at ten."

"I'll do what I can, Nils."

"Angels could do no more," Blixen said. "Good night, buddy."

"Good night."

Still pacing by the window, Sanderson said: "Nils, how do you plan to get out to the airport? Do you need a ride?"

"Not if it pulls you away from Isabel."

"She'd come along."

"Leave tio?" Blixen asked. "I think that's an awfully optimistic assumption. Or did you mean she'd bring Jesus with her?"

"This is going to surprise you," Sanderson said, "but she told me tonight that Jesus was beginning to get on her nerves a little. Well. Jesus, Gloria, the whole family."

Blixen stared at him for a while and then leaned back in his chair. "That *is* a surprise," he said.

"She started to talk about her work again, too," Sanderson said. "She's afraid Todd'll blackball her for staying out. She said she had to get away and think."

"She's not sneaking off anywhere alone," Blixen said. "Now I mean that, David."

"I understand, I understand. And so does she. We thrashed all that out. She still isn't convinced she's in real danger—or any *more* danger than any other Mexican in this bloodthirsty town is—but she accepts the fact that I'm worried and she's willing to respect my fears. She wants to go sailing—there's a marina at the foot of Sunflower that rents out sloops, little ones, Grunion class—and I finally said all right, all right, provided I could be with her."

"David, I don't like this."

"Right, naturally you don't like it!" Sanderson threw his hands in the air, let them slap against his sides. "Do you know what I feel like, Nils?" he demanded. "A Swiss negotiator who's finally wormed one piddling concession out of the South Vietnamese, only to hear the Cong say they don't like it. Do you realize how long I had to argue with that woman before I got even this much?"

Blixen cracked his knuckles. "What's a sloop?"

"Sloop's a small boat with one mast that's rigged with a mainsail and a jib."

Impressed, Blixen said: "And you can sail one of those things?"

"Blindfolded," Sanderson put his hands to the small of his back and gave a semishrug. "Actually, it's been a while. So I thought I'd go down early and practice a little. Isabel'll join me at two o'clock."

"Staying alone here in the meantime," Blixen said.

"Nils," Sanderson said, "I can't accompany her to the bathroom either. Can I? We'll all just have to grasp the nettle and take some chances. And what about Enid? Who tastes Enid's food? Who helps Enid across the street?"

"Call DeGroot and suggest that he assign a couple of deputies to Enid."

"You know what he'll say. He's got every spare man out now looking for the head and the hands to that body."

"Ask him anyhow."

"Speaking of heads, I wonder what they did with Holofernes's," Sanderson said half to himself.

Irritably Blixen said: "Now what are you talking about?"

"Holofernes."

"And who in God's name is Holofernes?"

"Holofernes?" Sanderson said. "Holofernes was an Assyrian general who laid siege to some Israelite town. So this nice Jewish girl dolled all up and swayed over to Holofernes's tent and indicated that she wouldn't mind fooling around a little. Well, she was a terrible liar—she wasn't at all what she seemed—so Holofernes never suspected he was nursing a viper in his bosom. He welcomed her, and that night, after he was asleep, this so-called nice Jewish girl took the general's sword and cut off his head. But I can't remember for the life of me what she did with it. . . . Well, it's not important."

"Are you through?" Blixen asked.

"All through," Sanderson said.

"What was this so-called nice Jewish girl's name? Delilah?"

"No," Sanderson said. "It was Judith."

CHAPTER TWENTY

A finger trailed across her lips. "Isabel?" someone coaxed. "Wake up."

She opened one sluggish eye.

Mrs. Billroth hovered beside the bed in a purple pants suit with a plate of hot buttered scones in one hand. The smell of honey and baked bread and tea floated in the air.

"I have died, haven't I," Isabel said, "and gone to heaven. Are those scones?"

"These are scones," said Mrs. Billroth. "Do you like scones?"

"I would kill for a scone," Isabel said. She reached for one, but the icy air outside her blankets fell across her warm bare arm like a branding iron, and she jerked her hand back and shoved it under her behind, shivering. "My *God,* Enid, it's cold in here!"

"I know it. I've got every heater in the place on and I still can't get warm. It's the wind. Well, we'll have a good sail."

"Sail!" Isabel hollered. "I forgot about the sail!" She jumped up, shot back under the covers again. "Where's David?"

"David left about an hour ago. How's your head?"

"Feels okay."

"Then David says we're supposed to meet him at two."

"Yes . . . 'We'?"

"He made me promise to bring you down and then he told Gloria to sit with her mom because he said I had to come out with you on the sloop. I said, why, I would not, I said I hated the water, I didn't even like to *drink* water, and he said that didn't matter because DeGroot wouldn't let his men play nursemaid, whatever that means."

"Yeah, I know what it means," Isabel said. "DeGroot won't guard us, so David's decided to."

"Back to that again," Mrs. Billroth said.

"Well, Blixen's got him just scared to death about the strychnine and all," Isabel said. "Don't blame David."

"I never heard anything so dippy in my life," said Mrs. Billroth.

"I know, I know."

"The one place I never will feel safe is on the ocean. I'm bound to get sick."

"No, you won't."

"Well, if I do, I know who I'll get sick *on*."

"Poor David," Isabel laughed.

"And here's another thing," Mrs. Billroth said. "Suppose some nut *is* after one of us, or both of us—can you imagine a better place for him to try something than out on a sloop in the middle of the Pacific Ocean?"

"We won't be out in the middle of the Pacific Ocean. David's a very cautious sailor."

"Sure," Mrs. Billroth said darkly, "if David's what he claims he is."

"Darling," Isabel said, "there are certain people in this world you just have to trust. Like swains and policemen."

"Oh, I know it," Mrs. Billroth grumbled. "I know . . ." While Isabel reluctantly inched out of bed and into a robe, Mrs. Billroth walked to the window and raised the blind on the brittle, blue, windy day. "I'll tell you this, though," she said, "if I end up out there murdered, I'll never forgive that man."

"Don't blame you a bit," Isabel said. "What time is it? David left his watch. It's on the bureau."

Mrs. Billroth consulted it. "You've got twenty minutes," she said.

"Hell," Isabel said. She grabbed up a scone and hurried toward the bathroom, dripping honey and crumbs behind her. "Sorry about that, Enid. I'll clean it up."

"I suppose that's why my mother always said what she did," Mrs. Billroth told her. "She was such a neat one."

"What did your mother always say?"

"People who live in glass houses should never eat scones," said Mrs. Billroth.

****

They parked the car in the marina lot and walked out between two lines of wind-whipped pennants to the end of a small wharf, where a number of neat, bobbing rental sloops were berthed.

"My goodness, did you ever see anything tinier in your life?" Mrs. Billroth asked. "Do we have to get into one of those?"

"It'll hold us," Isabel said. She shaded her eyes with one hand and waved wildly with the other. "There's David! Da-VID!"

A white pretty boat was slicing jauntily toward them through the choppy water. Sanderson sat in the back, apple-cheeked and excited. "Ahoy, shipmates!" he yelled thinly.

"Oh, for pity's sake," Mrs. Billroth muttered.

"Now don't spoil everything, Enid," Isabel said. "He's happy. Let him think he's saving us."

Expertly Sanderson brought the sloop almost to their feet. "Hi! Have you been waiting long?"

"Just drove up."

"Well, hop in! I pay by the hour."

"Have you been having fun, darling?"

"Ah, babe, I think I'll turn pirate. I nearly capsized once, but I stretched out until I was just hanging on by my heels and I saved her."

"That's it," Mrs. Billroth said.

"Enid? Enid!"

"No, you two go ahead. I'll just—"

"Enid, you climb in here," Isabel ordered. "Hurry up! This is costing us a fortune and we're going to enjoy ourselves or know the reason why."

"Shall I tell you the reason why?" Mrs. Billroth asked.

"Give me your hand, Enid," Sanderson said.

"Don't pull! Just—I'll—"

"Is she in?"

"Are you in, Enid?"

"There's water in this boat! The floor's covered with water!"

"There's always a little water," Isabel soothed. "Here's a nice can, dear. Bail."

"Everybody set?" Sanderson cried. "Shove off, mate!"

Isabel shoved.

****

The sun warmed her; the crack and bellying of the mainsail mesmerized her. "David," she said, "do you know what we ought to do when we grow up? Run away to sea."

"We'll do it, babe," Sanderson said.

"Are we to China yet?" Mrs. Billroth asked. They'd fixed a place for her low in the stern, well away from the swinging boom, where she sat like a paralyzed yogi.

"If you'd open your eyes, Enid," Isabel advised, "you wouldn't feel so ill."

"When I open my eyes," snapped Mrs. Billroth, "I see the horizon. Up and down, up and down. I know what I'm doing. Let me out at Hawaii. I'll fly back."

"Do you know how far we've come?" Sanderson asked. "We're barely down to the estuary. There's Brouwer's church."

"You're kidding," Mrs. Billroth said. "Tell me you're kidding. We must have been out here an hour and a half."

"Fifteen minutes," Isabel said. "It's twenty past two."

"Oh, God," said Mrs. Billroth.

"Look, there's Alfred in the vestry window," Isabel said.

"Where?"

"Isn't that Alfred? Can we sail up there, David?"

"Sure."

They swung into the estuary, faltered, found the wind again. They drifted under the bridge, past the narrow, white church. "No, that isn't Alfred," Sanderson said. "Is it?"

The dark figure at the window was unmoving.

"Alfred!" Isabel hollered. "Hoo-hoo!"

"I think he waved," Sanderson said.

"Well, why doesn't he come out and say hello?"

"Oh, you know Alfred."

"Yes, and I know something else," Mrs. Billroth suddenly said. She had opened her eyes and was craning her head at the estuary banks. "If anybody ever wanted to take a pot shot at a sitting duck, this is the place."

"Nobody's going to take any pot shots," Sanderson said.

"Well, you're the one who keeps—"

"But we'll go back anyway," Sanderson said.

The figure at the window was still there, still undefinable, as they circled lazily and tacked back under the bridge toward the bay.

"I hope he's all right," Isabel said in a worried tone.

"Who?" Mrs. Billroth asked. She'd closed her eyes again.

"Alfred."

"Oh, you know Alfred," Mrs. Billroth said. "Let's just get away from these banks."

"She's right, Captain," Isabel said. "Tote that rudder, lift that sail. You know what her mother always says."

"What?" Sanderson asked.

"A rolling stern gathers no moss . . ."

****

They were visited by a lugubrious seagull, which prompted Sanderson to recite all he could remember of "The Ancient Mariner," which was plenty, with gestures. They hove to at a waterside caterer's and bought two box lunches. Two, because Mrs. Billroth insisted she couldn't gag down a morsel, although she made away with half of Isabel's before she was finished. They dreamed and grew sunburned and very tired. And finally, at ten minutes to five, they returned to the colorful wharf and paid for the boat and headed happily toward the parking lot.

And it was here that they first heard the news.

They caught it on the attendant's portable radio just inside the gate.

That afternoon, while they'd been sailing and dreaming and burning and laughing, Dr. Harold Trout had killed himself.

CHAPTER TWENTY-ONE

Blixen was in a projection room with Barney Lewis, viewing a color-corrected answer print, when Sanderson's call reached him. "Trout did *what?*" he exclaimed.

Barney touched the microphone switch and said: "Hold it, Alex," to the projectionist.

"Killed himself," Sanderson said.

The film flickered to a stop; the house lights came on.

"I don't believe it," Blixen said. *"Trout?"* It wouldn't penetrate; he couldn't disengage himself from the lurid fictional world Saul Stagg had been racing through.

"I know how you feel," Sanderson began, "we all had the—"

"David, wait a minute. Where did you hear this?"

"It's been on the radio."

"But did you check it yourself?"

"He did it in his apartment, Nils. DeGroot and his men are all over the place."

Blixen puffed out his cheeks and let his head fall against the high leather back of the projection-room seat. "All right. What happened?"

"Well, as nearly as they can reconstruct it," Sanderson said, "sometime after two-thirty, he locked all his windows and his door, made himself a drink in his sitting room, turned the gas on, and lay down on his couch."

"Gas? That's what killed him?"

"That's what they presume. There'll be an inquest."

"And he was in his sitting room?"

"Right."

"Unvented heater?"

"Yes, unvented. All the apartments have them."

"How do they know it wasn't an accident, David?"

"Oh, he couldn't have missed the smell. And the gas tap was

turned full on. So a draft couldn't have blown the flame out. He had to turn the heater off and then turn it on again, all the way."

Presently, Blixen said: "Did he leave a note?"

"They haven't found one."

"Any survivors?"

"Not a soul."

"Where does his money go?"

"Cancer research. If there *is* any money. He was barely scraping along, Nils." Sanderson laughed a little. "Why? What are you looking for, a murder motive? I can promise you he wasn't murdered. They had to break the door down to get in."

"Yale lock?"

"Dead lock, key on the inside—*and* a bolt."

"Had he been to the morgue?"

"What?"

"He was due at the morgue this afternoon," Blixen said, "to try to identify the body in the barrel."

"Oh. No, he never made it."

"So we still don't know who the man was."

"No," Sanderson said. "DeGroot's been looking for some X rays Trout had promised to dig up, but there's no sign of them. He's more convinced than ever that the corpse is Junkin."

"It can't be Junkin."

"I hope not, for Jesus Mary's sake."

"Where was Jesus, by the way, this afternoon?"

"In a bar on B Street. With a bartender and six other customers. He got there at two, and he left at half-past four."

Blixen transferred the phone to his other ear. "How was two-thirty established as the suicide time, David?"

"Well," Sanderson said, "that's when Trout was last seen alive. So it would be two-thirty or later. Closer to two-thirty than to three, according to the coroner."

"Seen alive by whom?"

"A hell of a reliable witness. DeGroot. He dropped by to drive Trout to the morgue. But Trout seemed preoccupied, worried, and told him to come back later. He said he had company."

"What company?"

"DeGroot didn't know. When he did come back, Trout was dead."

"Where were you all this time?"

"Sailing with Isabel and Enid. We got in around five."

"Incidentally, did you have a chance to ask Isabel about the Mexican visitor from Mazatlan?"

"I did, and she doesn't recall seeing him. So I asked Jesus Mary, I asked Gloria, Enid, Judith, I even asked Cabral. Everybody drew a blank."

"Cabral's back then," Blixen said.

"Cabral got back about twenty minutes ago. He'd been after grunion."

"Catch any?"

"Couple of sacks full."

Blixen gave a start. "Really?"

"Well, he had help," Sanderson said. "He took a friend along, an army chaplain. Cabral doesn't have a car. The chaplain drove."

"Well, I'll be damned." Blixen studied the white empty screen at the foot of the narrow room. "David, I'd like to know where everybody else was at two-thirty. Could you find that out for me?"

"Now, by everybody—"

"By everybody, I guess I mean Judy, Gloria, and Brouwer."

"Well, Gloria was with Judith at the restaurant."

"They both confirm this?"

"Both confirm it."

"And Brouwer?"

"Brouwer was writing a sermon. In his church."

"Was he alone?"

"Yes."

"Well, then, how do you know—"

"We saw him," Sanderson said. "We were down by the estuary, and Isabel noticed Alfred in the vestry window, so we sailed up past the bridge and yelled at him."

"Did he come out?"

"No. I asked him later why he hadn't, and he said he hadn't even heard us. Too absorbed."

"And what time was this?"

"This was about two-twenty."

"Well—he could still have walked uptown after you left."

"No," Sanderson said. "We sailed around for a while in the bay and one or another of us had an eye on that church until at least three, and nobody left."

Blixen sighed and sat up. "All right, David," he said, "thank you. I'm terribly sorry about Trout."

"It was a terrible thing."

"How's everybody taking it?"

"It's pretty well wiped us all out, I think."

"Of course."

"Listen, Nils, what time do you want us to pick you up? You said your plane left at ten?"

"Right. Well, I'll be stalled here for another two hours, at least. . . . How about eight?"

"We'll be there."

"I'll see you then."

"Goodbye, Nils."

"Goodbye, David."

He numbly replaced the receiver on its hook.

"Nils," Barney Lewis said, "why don't we cut this short? I can check it out tomorrow. You look a little shook up."

"I'm all right, I'll be fine."

"Nothing stranger to hear than half a conversation," Barney said. "I—heard you say suicide . . ."

Blixen nodded.

"How?"

"They're not sure of the details."

"Probably never will be now."

"Oh, there's one person who could tell us."

"Who's that?"

"His murderer," Blixen said.

CHAPTER TWENTY-TWO

Blixen was waiting near the studio gate, talking to the night guard, when Sanderson pulled his ramshackle Cadillac to the curb and tooted.

"Noah, I'll see you Monday," Blixen said.

"Good luck back there," said the guard. "Sell 'em now. We need the business. They're tough boys."

"I'll dazzle 'em with my footwork," Blixen promised. "They'll never lay a glove on me."

"Way to go," Noah said.

Blixen opened the Cadillac's back door and tossed his overnight bag in. In front, Isabel slid close to Sanderson. "There's room up here, Nils." She waved at the guard. "Hi, Noah!"

"Hi, sweetheart," Noah called. "I've missed you. Where have you been?"

"Oh . . ."

"Huh?"

"Oh, around," Isabel said. She plaited her fingers in her lap and sat frowning down at them while Blixen squeezed in next to her and slammed his door and Sanderson catapulted them all back into the endless Los Angeles traffic.

"So where's Enid?" Blixen inquired.

"I told you that'd be the first thing he'd ask," Sanderson said. "Not even a hello."

"Enid wouldn't come," Isabel said.

"Why not?"

"She said the Toonerville Trolley looked safer to her than this car. She said David takes her courage too much for granite. She claims her life was just a bowl of Cheerios until David came along with his engines of destruction. DeGroot's watching her."

"She also told me I'd become a milestone around her neck," Sanderson said. "Was I right to feel flattered?"

"You made that up," Blixen said.

"I swear on my mother's grave that's what she said, milestone," Sanderson insisted. "Didn't she, babe?"

Smiling, Isabel nodded. "Once she was waiting table and she spilled a dish of refried beans into a customer's lap. I asked her if he'd bawled her out, and she said he sure as hell had, he'd really raped her over the coals."

Their laughter filled the car, warm, relaxed, intimate.

Like the old days, Blixen thought. *An ice-age ago last week . . .*
Each of them fell silent.

The tires hummed hypnotically; on either side of them cars shot past like bullets.

"Dollar for your thoughts, babe," Sanderson said.

"Pretty inflated prices."

"Pretty inflated times."

"I don't know," Isabel said, "I was just thinking that we always used to laugh like that."

"So was I," Sanderson said.

"David," Blixen said, "what's the word on the Trout autopsy?"

"They'll hold it tomorrow," Sanderson answered.

"The missing X rays ever show up?"

"Not yet."

"I'll bet they never find out who the man in the barrel was now," Isabel said.

"No marks anywhere on the body to give an indication of his background?"

"Nothing," Sanderson said. "He might have been a manual laborer, he might have been a college professor. They just can't tell."

"That's what the hands might have revealed," Blixen said.

"Occupation? Yes, maybe . . ."

Thoughtfully, Blixen said: "Isabel—you know the garnet ring Gloria wears . . ."

"Something's happened to that ring," Isabel said. "I noticed she didn't have it on today."

"Was she very fond of it?"

"Crazy about it."

"Where'd she get it?"

"It was a birthday present. It came last January."

"Birthday present from whom?"

"Well, that's the mystery," Isabel said. "Nobody knows. Or at least *I* don't know. Somebody in Mexico. Mazatlan."

"Secret admirer?"

"You got me."

"Relative?"

"No," Isabel said, "I wouldn't think it was a relative. The whole thing baffled Jude, too, and she'd know if there were any relatives in Mazatlan."

"Judith ever spend any time in Mazatlan herself?"

"Oh, sure, years. That's where she met Jesus Mary."

"No kidding."

"Yeah, he was in the union there, organizing the dock workers or something. One look and pow. The funny thing is that Jude was going with this other guy at the time."

"American?"

"No, Mexican. Jude always did dig Mexican men."

"I suppose he lived in Mazatlan, too," Blixen said. "The first boyfriend."

"Uh-huh, he was a local boxer, big favorite."

"Tall fellow, probably," Blixen speculated, "like Jesus Mary."

"Well, that was the funny part," Isabel said. "He wasn't. He must have been the only short man Jude ever went with."

"Can you recall his name?"

"Why? He's not boxing anymore. He'd be about fifty now."

"I just thought I might have seen him once."

"Oh—Rafael Morales?"

"Morales . . ."

"I don't think he ever got to the States," Isabel said.

"When was all this happening?" Blixen asked.

"This was around 1946, '47 . . . Jude and Jesus were married on Christmas Day, '47, so it was before that." Isabel turned to peer at him quizzically. "Why? What's—"

"Kids," Sanderson broke in, "I hate to interrupt this fascinating conversation, but I don't know which airline to head for."

"TWA," Blixen said pensively. "Please . . ."

CHAPTER TWENTY-THREE

They checked Blixen's one bag downstairs and then all three of them trooped through the weapons-control gate and up the stairs to the lounge for a drink.

It was crowded and noisy in the bar but Sanderson managed to find them a small table by the window. "So," he said. "What'll we have?"

"Scotch and water," Blixen said.

"Same here," Isabel said. "Or anything. Whatever."

"Don't move. I'll be right back."

On the field, a huge plane came lumbering down the runway, wing lights blinking.

"Big one," Isabel said.

"It's a 747."

They watched it gain speed and heave reluctantly into the polluted night.

"Boy, I wish I was going with you," Isabel murmured.

"To New *York?* You can't mean it."

"To anywhere. Just away." She rested her cheek on her hand. "I get so tired of always . . ." Her voice trailed off.

"Of always what?"

"I don't know. Holding the world together . . ."

Blixen smiled.

Isabel lifted her brows. "You didn't realize I possessed such enormous power, did you?"

"Never till now."

"It's funny, though," Isabel said, "there was a time when I really believed it."

"Maybe there was a time when it was really true."

"Not bloody likely."

"Why not? Worlds expand. This isn't the same world you lived in when you were twelve, Isabel. Or six. Or two."

She weighed the idea, tearing paper matches out of a folder one by one and piling them in the ashtray.

"What was your mother like?" Blixen asked.

"Oh, Christ, wild," Isabel said.

"In what way?"

"Well. If there'd been a Kit-Kat Klub in Nayarit, she'd have been a chorine in it. Great dancer, great legs. Loved the boys. Pretty little thing." Seriously Isabel added: "I take after Papa's side."

"Were you friends, you and your mother?"

"Were we *friends?* We were related. Of course we were friends."

"Would you have been friends if you hadn't been related?"

More matches joined the pile. "Yeah—I think so. She was beautiful—and I felt sorry for her. That's not a bad basis for a friendship, is it?"

"Practically classic."

"I never saw anybody who could go to pieces quicker in a crisis," Isabel said. "I grew up thinking that's what you got to do if you were pretty, go to pieces."

"Then no doubt your dad would put everything straight."

"*I'd* put everything straight. My dad couldn't straighten a ruler. My dad was—" Fretfully she tore the empty match folder in half and tossed it onto the mound of matches. "Well, let's not get into *that,*" she said.

"So you more or less ran the household in those days," Blixen suggested.

"I sure did."

"More or less held the world together?"

After a moment, Isabel muttered: "Well, touché, as the villain cried when he cut the hero's head off." She sprawled back in her chair, staring out at the busy field. Presently she said: "How come you're being so patient with me, *patrón?*" She dug her chin into her chest. "I don't mean *patrón.* Do you object to *hombre?*"

"I don't object to *patrón,*" Blixen said, "if there's love in it."

"I've given you a couple of bad days lately, haven't I?"

"Bad for me because they've been bad for you, that's all," Blixen said.

"I can assure you of one thing though. I'm not just being arbitrary about this—I'm not just throwing my weight around to see who I can hurt."

"I understand."

"This has been the most important year of my life. Working in the series. Working with you. Learning my trade. I'll never, never forget it. But I'll never forget what I've seen in Ramona County, either."

"I hope you don't."

"I was telling you the exact simple truth when I said I had to fight back. And if that hurts you—or the series—in any way whatsoever, then I'm sorry. But it can't be helped."

Blixen folded his arms, reflecting. "Isabel," he said at last, "do you approve of the character you play in *Stagg?*"

"Of the character? Certainly."

"Do your Chicano friends approve?"

"Very much."

"And do you realize how many millions of people are seeing a true Chicana now for the first time in their lives because of that program? How many—"

But she was shaking her head energetically. "No, no, no, no, no!" she interrupted. "I won't—"

"It's true."

"It may be true, but it isn't enough! No television show can change a bigot, *patrón!* Fear changes bigots! I can't reach out of the tube and threaten them! Strangle them! My place is with Jesus Mary."

"Or behind him."

"The point—" She stirred. "Or what?"

Blixen leaned forward. "Isabel, I've thought about this problem a great deal. And I have something to suggest to you. I don't ask you to believe me. Just to listen. Will you do that?"

She shut her mouth, drawn again to the window.

"Are you listening?"

"Yes!"

"I want you to consider a plot. An actress, used to holding the world together, is given a secondary role in a show. But because of the extent of her talent, it isn't long before she's outshining the star, carrying the program by herself."

"Oh, please."

"Recognize her?"

"I don't know whether you're talking about me or not. But if you are—"

"I am."

"Then don't be ridiculous. I don't carry *Stagg.*"

"Are you still listening?"

"I'm *listening!*"

"There's just one cloud on the actress's horizon," Blixen continued, "but it's been there all her life. She's stronger than her parents. She's cleverer than her mother, more successful than her father. She constantly tries to convince them that this isn't so, because she's afraid the truth will hurt them. But it's a hard fact to conceal. Sometimes her drive to succeed is so strong that she succeeds in spite of herself. Yet every time that happens, she pays for it. Her mother cries. Her father topples."

Isabel had turned to stare fixedly at him.

"Still recognize the actress?" Blixen asked.

"She's gotten younger."

"How old is she now?"

"Twelve. Who told you about Texas?"

"Donald Gould."

"I'll have to have a talk with Donald."

"How long after your father's death was it before you tried acting again?"

"I don't remember."

"Years?"

"What are you implying? That I blamed myself when my dad was shot?"

"Did you?"

"Of course not!"

"Why did you stop acting then?"

"I had to. We moved away from that town."

"No radio station in your new town?"

"There was no time. I had to go to school."

"Private school?"

"Yes!"

"Who paid for it? Uncle Jesus?"

"I see Donald laid the whole thing on you. That's what I get for confiding in a gossip."

"All right, let's consider the little girl's new life," Blixen said. "Suddenly she doesn't have a worry in the world. Now there's a different man to measure herself against, and this man doesn't topple. This man is *machismo* itself—general of the armies—and all any general demands is obedience from the troops. In exchange for marching along like a good soldier, the little girl receives security and protection and love. And in this benign atmosphere all the old wounds begin to heal. A part comes along in a little theater production. She takes it. She's offered another, and she takes that. She grows up, moves to East L.A., does some shows in Spanish repertory, takes a bit part in *Bonanza* for the fun of it, lands a *Gunsmoke*—and before long finds herself in a series called *Stagg at Bay*."

"You know what we need here?" Isabel asked. "Ralph Edwards holding up this big book with 'This is Your Life, Isabel Chavez,' written on it in gold letters. Then you could haul out all my old teachers, my first boyfriend—"

"She's given," Blixen said, "a secondary role in *Stagg*. But because of the extent of her talent, it isn't long before she's outshining the star, carrying the program by herself."

"I wonder what's happened to our boy?" Isabel stretched her neck, looking for Sanderson.

"Do you understand the point I'm trying to make, Isabel?"

"It couldn't be neater, *patrón*. It's a pity it isn't valid."

"No parallel between twelve and twenty-three, in your opinion?"

"You've boxed yourself in, *patrón*. You need my weak little father to make your parallel, and the poor man's dead."

"Fathers never die," Blixen said. "That's the trouble with fathers."

"Mine died."

"And your psyche resurrects him every time it needs a new scarecrow to run from."

Isabel ceased scanning the bar to look at him. "Oh, really."

"Really."

"And who have I picked for my weak father-figure this time? David? You?"

"How about Murf?"

Isabel's jaw dropped. "Murf?" She gave a short yelp of laughter. "Murphy *Smith*? What kind of a father-figure is this?"

"What kind was your own?"

Isabel stared at him. "Well—*yes*, but still—"

"We're talking about a weak man in a position of authority, aren't we. Now. What do you expect is going to happen to Murf when he grasps the fact that you're the real star of the series?"

Isabel returned to her mutilated matches; a thin glaze of perspiration shaded the sides of her nose.

"Shall I tell you what's going to happen to him?" Blixen prodded.

"No."

"Nothing."

Presently Isabel glanced up.

"Absolutely nothing," Blixen said. "Because he'll never grasp it. He's not smart enough to grasp it. And even if he were, he's too egotistical to accept it. You can't hold his world together any more than you can destroy it. You have no effect on it whatsoever. No more effect than you had on your first father's world. Your success didn't kill your father; it won't harm Murf."

Hoarsely Isabel said: "Listen, I don't have to sit here—"

"I'm almost through." Blixen took one of her cold hands in both of his. "Isabel, your talent dumbfounds me. I've never seen a young player with more power, fewer mannerisms, less to learn. You're good now; you're going to be phenomenal. *Stagg* can give you polish, but you'll go far beyond *Stagg,* far beyond Murf or Donald, far beyond most of your contemporaries. *Provided* you stop running from those scarecrows."

Barely moving her lips, Isabel said: "You can't admit that I might be running *toward* something, can you?"

"Forward's fine," Blixen said. "Run forward as hard as you can. But you don't have to abandon acting for political commitment. They're not incompatible."

"Isn't that something for me to decide?"

"It's something for you to think long and hard about *before* deciding."

"Okay, here we go," Sanderson said behind them. He came cheerfully squeezing through the crowd with a highball in each hand. "Where's my chair?"

"Stolen," Blixen reported. "Where's your drink?"

"I changed my mind when I figured out that I couldn't carry three glasses," Sanderson said. "Too many calories anyway."

Isabel stood up. "You are so right. I didn't want one in the first place. *Hasta la vista, patrón.* Don't let the New York muggers get you." She started sideways through the packed room toward the door.

"Hey, babe?" Sanderson called.

"Come on, David. I'm tired."

"Well—but—"

"Go ahead, David," Blixen said. "I'll see you Saturday."

"Well, I thought I'd wait until the plane took off."

"Go, go!"

Befuddled, Sanderson eased into the press of bodies. "Babe?"

But Isabel wouldn't look around.

CHAPTER TWENTY-FOUR

Blixen was seated on a green leather bench near the departure gate when the public-address announcer intoned his name and directed him to go to one of the white courtesy telephones.

He found one in the hallway beside the candy counter. "This is Nils Blixen," he said. "You have a call for me?"

The operator asked him to wait, please, and soon Schreiber came on, breathing hard. "Oh, good," he said. "They caught you."

"There's been some delay on the field," Blixen informed him. "Are you all right, Wade? You sound—"

"I just this minute heard from Bliss."

"Who's Bl— Oh. Well?"

"Okay, there *was* a paternity suit filed against Jesus Mary Chavez in Bliss County, Texas, on October 5, 1954."

"Yes?"

"But the case never came to trial. Guess why."

"I give up."

"Guess."

"The mother turned out to be a man?"

"You're not far wrong at that. Except that it was the reverse of that coin. The father turned out *not* to be a man."

"The—what?"

"Well, that's not fair," Schreiber said. "The suit was dismissed because the defendant happened to have an irrefutable alibi. Medical records proved that Jesus Mary had been sterile since his mid-teens."

"*Did* they," Blixen murmured.

"Well?" Schreiber asked after a second or two. "Does that confirm it? You told me you had some crazy idea—"

"It's confirmed."

"You also told me," Schreiber added, "that you'd let me in on it if I came back with the right answer."

"I was checking up on DeGroot."

"On— Why? What did DeGroot do?"

"DeGroot got carried away," Blixen said, "when he was trying to convince me of what a bastard Jesus Mary was. He claimed Jesus Mary had a criminal record as long as your arm. I doubted it. So I—"

"Why would you doubt that?"

"Jesus Mary's a Mexican national. Do you think the Immigration Department would allow him to stay here if he'd been convicted of any crimes?"

"Well, he's a Communist," Schreiber pointed out. "They haven't deported him for that."

"Who says he's a Communist?"

"*He* does!"

"He also claims he's a father."

"True," Schreiber said slowly. "Very true."

"Rule of thumb number thirty-eight," Blixen said. " 'Beware the man who's manly every minute.' "

"So our Jesus Mary's been dissembling a little," Schreiber mused.

"More than a little."

"Can't have been altogether a picnic for his wife."

"His wife," Blixen said, "is a living catalog of psychosomatic illnesses."

"Figures."

"Some of which," Blixen went on, "are the result of frustration. Some of which come from guilt."

"I can't see what *she's* got to be guilty about."

"She bore her sterile husband a daughter named Gloria. Was it a virgin birth?"

"Maybe Gloria was born before the wedding."

"No," Blixen said, "she was born thirteen months after the wedding."

"Peyton Place West, for God's sake," Schreiber said. "I wonder if Gloria knows."

"I have an idea she does," Blixen said. "I think she got a ring from her real father on her last birthday. She's very undecided about that gift. She loves it—and she's ashamed of it."

"You sound as though you know who the father is."

"I believe I do."

"Well?"

"I think he was a fighter named Rafael Morales. He lived in Mazatlan."

"Lived? Is he dead?"

Two stewardesses strode down the hall and into the departure tunnel; a number of passengers had begun to drift furtively toward the gate. "That's something else you can determine for me, Wade," Blixen said. "Find out if Morales left Mazatlan recently. He was a well-known figure. You shouldn't have any trouble locating people who knew him. Start with the boxing promoters."

"You want me to go *down* there?"

"Yes, I do."

"Well, Nils, you aren't my only client! I can't simply—"

"I'll be at the Warwick. Call me tomorrow night. If Morales has disappeared, go to the Mazatlan boxing commission and get his medical records—particularly torso X rays—and take them back to De-Groot. Got all that?"

"Distressed, Schreiber said: "Morales—Mazatlan—boxing commission . . ."

"Good. They're calling my flight. I'll see you."

"But—!"

"Thanks, buddy."

CHAPTER TWENTY-FIVE

The studio had sent a car to Kennedy to pick him up, and by half past seven he had reached his hotel, registered, and been shown to his room. He showered and shaved, and then sat in an overstuffed tan chair by the window, looking out at the apple-crisp morning, lost in thought, until his telephone rang.

It was Todd, as high-strung as a master mariner who smells port just over the horizon. "By God, you're here," he said. "I can't believe it."

"No more can I," Blixen said.

"How was your flight?"

"A little violent over America's heartland, Arthur, but apart from that, very pleasant."

"Speaking of throwing up," Todd said, "have you read the papers?"

"Not yet."

"Connaught's at it again. He made another anti-TV speech in the House. He said he was going to purge the filth and sadism out of American television if he had to impeach the entire FCC. He likened himself to Jesus driving the money-changers from the temple. He said he was no longer going to let the perverts press down upon the brows of children this crown of thorns. He said we shall not crucify innocence upon this cross of dirt. The gallery applauded for thirteen minutes."

"There's our next President, Arthur."

"Jesus Christ, you'd joke about your own mother's death."

"Who's joking?"

"Well," Todd said, "anyway, the networks are crazy with fear. It's a terrible thing to see grown men tremble. So we got our work cut out for us, boy. I'd say our chances right now are about forty-sixty against renewal. Of course, that could change. I've got a couple of little notions I want to throw at you."

"That's what I was afraid of."

"Don't drag your feet, sonny, it ain't the time. Are you dressed?"

"I'm dressed."

"Come on up. Top floor. I don't recall the suite number. Ask somebody."

Sighing, Blixen put on a tie and made his way to the top floor, where a bellman pointed out Todd's suite to him. The door was opened by an associate of Todd's named Flanders, a portly, worried youngster who had only recently joined the company and who was on his first New York selling trip. "God, we're in trouble, Nils," Flanders said. "I don't know whether we'll be able to pull this one out or not, I really don't—"

"Where's—?"

"Nils!" Todd bellowed from the sitting room.

"Yoh!"

"Don't come in for a minute!"

Blixen glanced questioningly at Flanders.

"We've made up some graphs and pictures and junk," Flanders said. "He wants to set 'em up for you."

"Graphs and pictures and junk couldn't sell milk to a baby."

"*You* know that, and *I* know that—"

"Okay, come ahead!" Todd boomed. The sitting-room door was thrust open. Todd, swathed in a wine-colored dressing gown, raced back to an easel and stood alertly beside it. "First tell me how close you have to get before you can read the thing."

Blixen stopped. "Right here."

"Read it."

"Stagg at Bay," Blixen read aloud, "comparative share—"

"That's enough. How far away are you?"

Blixen squinted. "Thirty feet."

"Shoot," Todd complained. "Anybody in the back row of that conference room tomorrow ain't gonna see a thing." He glared at Flanders. "I told you to make 'em bigger!"

"I'd say the easel's further away than that," Flanders said. "Um—closer to forty feet."

"Listen," Todd said, "I'll grant you this gentleman can't produce pictures worth beans, but don't you challenge his eye. If he says thirty feet, it's thirty feet."

Waves of blood had begun to surge into Flanders's face. "Why, I never said he couldn't produce—"

"Go ahead, measure it, measure it," Todd ordered impatiently.

Flanders turned to Blixen. "I swear I never said—"

"That's all right, Dwayne," Blixen said mildly. "I'll get you some-day. I don't forget."

Flanders chuckled a little and Blixen smiled back and Flanders tapped the gold wedding ring on his left hand against a marble table-top and said: "I'll fetch the tape, okay?" and walked off.

"Come look at this, Nils," Todd said. "If this don't fake 'em out of their socks, nothing will."

Blixen approached the easel. "What's the main curve?"

"That's fan mail," Todd explained. "This next graph shows how far we've bounced back after each blockbuster movie."

"What happens if they ask about seasonal share average?"

"Well, you just kind of mumble your way around that one. Here's—"

"*I* mumble my way around it?" Blixen asked.

"Well, you're the one they come to hear, boy," Todd said win-ningly. "I mean, who knows the show better than you do?"

"Arthur, this kind of stuff isn't going to change any minds."

"Oh, hell, I know it," Todd said. "But it looks *good,* don't it? It looks sincere."

"And we're nothing if not sincere."

"Right," Todd said. "So—anyway—you show 'em the graphs, you promise 'em the far locations, the super guest stars, you eliminate the violence, and all you ask in return is a little more advertising and a different time slot. Are we agreed?"

"When does this search for truth and beauty come off?"

"We're set for conference room B at eleven tomorrow morning. Now I've oiled the troubled waters as much as I can. I *think* I've smoothed Seacliff's feathers. He likes the show and he carries a lot of weight over there. He's not the final word, but he's close to it. We're having dinner with him and Sheila tonight."

"I'm surprised you'd trust me at another party with Norman."

"I pondered long and hard about that," Todd admitted, "and then I thought, ah, what the hell, let's go for broke. I also thought if you started another fight, maybe I could kill you before too much damage was done."

"Thirty feet one inch," Flanders said bleakly. He was on his hands and knees below them, pressing one end of a yellow tape measure against the easel. He sat back. "Well—wrong again."

"Ah, don't fret about it," Todd said. "At least you're a good judge of producin' talent." He lumbered toward the bedroom. "I'm gonna get dressed."

Eyes shut, Flanders waited until the bedroom door slammed, and then he sucked air deeply in through his nose and let it out his mouth. "You know," he said, "that man has a very destructive sense of humor?" He looked at Blixen. "Let me explain what happened—"

The ringing telephone stopped him. He climbed to his feet and picked up the receiver. "Mr. Todd's suite," he said. He listened, eyeing Blixen. "Yes, he is," he said. "Who wants to speak to him?" Lowering the phone, he muttered: "Sanders, or something like that? Samson?"

"Oh . . ." Blixen took the phone and walked with it to the window. "Yes, David."

The connection was deplorable. Faintly Sanderson said: ". . . all over the hotel for you—DeGroot's . . ."

"David? Hold it. I can't hear."

"Is that better?" Sanderson shouted weakly.

"Not much. What's your number? I'll call you back."

"I'll holler! I can hear *you!* We can't waste the time! It's DeGroot again—"

"Oh, for Christ's sake, David!"

"He's arrested Jesus!"

"For *murder?*"

"Possession of pot! One of the deputies found a marijuana plant growing on the hill behind the restaurant! The whole family's so mad they say they're going to spirit Jesus off to Mexico the minute he's sprung."

"That's ridiculous!"

"I know!"

"They don't mean it! They've—"

"Oh, I think they mean it, Nils! You ought to hear Isabel."

"Let me talk to Isabel!"

"Isabel isn't here. She went with the lawyer to raise bail. She says DeGroot's done this on purpose to keep Jesus around until the police can rig a frame! She says he's determined to nail Jesus for that murder if it's the last thing he ever does!"

"I'm afraid she's right."

"Of course she's right!"

"David, I'm going to call Teet. If I can convince Teet to drop the marijuana charge, do you think you can keep Isabel and the family there until I get back?"

"Oh, God, Nils, you're asking for the moon!"

"Try."

"I'll try," Sanderson shouted thinly, "but I promise nothing! You haven't seen them! It was like a madhouse around here when they hauled Jesus off!"

"Do your best."

"I'm sorry to have to load all this on your back, Nils! How's everything in New York?"

"Everything's fine. . . . Goodbye, David."

"Goodbye!"

Blixen depressed the receiver bar, then rang the hotel operator and asked her to connect him at once with DeGroot's office in Ramona City, California. He thought for a while, cradling the phone, then turned to see Todd in the bedroom doorway, zipping up his pants and looking tense.

"*Now* what?" Todd said.

"Just a little private business, Arthur. Don't panic."

"It's that *pachuca* beast again, right?"

"Right."

"Sonny," Todd warned, "if you foul up this Seacliff deal after everything I've put into it—if you—"

The telephone rang. Blixen snatched it up. "Hello!"

"Nils," DeGroot said as clearly as though he were in the next room. "Well, how are you, old-timer?" The bland voice flowed like warm oil into his ear. "What are you doing in New York? They did say New York, didn't they?"

"Teet, have you lost your mind!"

DeGroot chuckled. "So they called you."

"Of course they called me!"

"Yeah, I thought somebody might do that. Now who was right and who was wrong about the marijuana?"

"You don't give any more of a damn about the marijuana than I do!"

Again the chuckle came indulgently over the wire. "I don't?"

"Teet, what's the *point?* You can't hold him! He'll be on the street in twenty minutes!"

"Well, now," DeGroot said, "maybe twenty minutes'll be enough."

Blixen gripped the receiver. "Enough for what?"

"Hm?"

"Will you quit playing around?"

"Enough for Mrs. Junkin to identify the body in the morgue," DeGroot said.

Blixen exhaled explosively. "So she's finally agreed to come down."

"She's there now."

"Teet," Blixen asked, "when was the last time you were sued for false arrest?"

"I'm pleased to say that that's never happened to me yet, old-timer."

"Well, it'll sure as hell happen to you today," Blixen said, "the minute you try to charge Jesus Mary Chavez with the murder of George Junkin."

"Maybe I ought to tell you," DeGroot said, "that the district attorney's as convinced as I am. All in the world he's waiting for is a positive identification from Mrs. Junkin."

"He'll never get it. Junkin's alive."

A note of fatigue crept into the confident voice. "Nils . . ."

"He's in eastern Canada, Teet."

Presently DeGroot said: "Fine. Produce him."

"I will. Him or a deposition. I don't think he'll want to come home."

DeGroot was silent for a moment, breathing into the phone. "You sound awfully sure of yourself."

"I am. I've had a team of private investigators on it. Pep Cisneros's outfit."

"Pep," DeGroot repeated.

"Pep's a very good man."

"Um," DeGroot said. "Hang on." He covered the mouthpiece and asked someone in a muffled voice to check with the morgue about the Junkin body, and then he uncovered the phone and said: "You know so damned much—who was in the barrel?"

"I've been working on that, too. I'll have an answer for you to-night."

"Isn't it interesting how you always have to wait for an answer."

"I'll go this far," Blixen said. "I think I know why the head and the hands were cut off."

"Why?"

"I'll have to ask you not to mention this yet to the Chavez family."

"Why?"

"That's my condition, take it or leave it."

"You and your goddamn games . . ."

"Do you agree?" Blixen asked.

"Yes, yes. Go ahead."

"I think they would have given away his profession. I think he would have been identified in ten minutes. His hands had probably been broken a hundred times. The ears were cauliflowered. He was a boxer."

"Named what?"

"I'll tell you tonight."

"Nils, if you're withholding evidence . . . !"

"I'm withholding a surmise. The day they write a law against that, you tell me."

Another male voice rumbled in the California background, and DeGroot said: "Hang on, Nils," and covered the mouthpiece again.

Behind Blixen, Todd waited in the bedroom doorway with his head pushed forward and his fists on his hips. Flanders had vanished.

"Okay, sorry," DeGroot growled. "What were we saying?"

"We were saying that your best hedge against a false arrest suit would undoubtedly be to drop those ridiculous marijuana charges and offer an apology before—"

"Hey, hey, hey, hey," DeGroot said.

"Teet, you're skating on the thinnest ice I ever saw. What a good civil liberties lawyer could do to you for a trick like this boggles the mind. You've shown prejudice from the beginning. You have no proof that Jesus Mary planted the marijuana—or even knew it was there. You're betting every chip you own on the statement of an anxious, scared woman."

"I'll drop the charges," DeGroot said, "but I won't apologize."

"In other words, Mrs. Junkin couldn't confirm the identification."

"She wasn't sure."

"I'd apologize, Teet," Blixen said. "I really would."

"Just be advised of this: that son of a bitch better keep himself available, because if I catch him even *looking* toward Mexico, I'll slap a material-witness warrant on him—and I'll make it stick, buddy, don't think I won't."

"Why should he run? He's innocent."

"Sure he's innocent. *Stalin* was innocent."

"Where can I get in touch with you later?"

"I'll either be here in the office," DeGroot said, "or they'll know where to find me."

"I'll call you as soon as I have anything definite at all, Teet. And thank you."

"I must be losing my marbles," DeGroot said. "That's the only explanation."

The phone cracked in Blixen's ear and he jerked it away, grinning wryly as he replaced it.

"I hate it," Todd said, "when a tricky man smiles. I always end up getting screwed."

"Sorry, Arthur."

"*Have* I been screwed?"

"Not yet."

"Aaron's," Todd said. "Reservation's in my name, eight o'clock tonight. And by God, you better be there."

"I'll be there," Blixen said, smiling.

CHAPTER TWENTY-SIX

It was a wide, white and gold room, rich with cascading draperies and silver wine carts. Lights blazed in the ceiling chandeliers; menus were meant to be read here, food to be seen. Six female fiddlers stood one above the other on a curved staircase and played Debussy, eyes and teeth and rings shining with every soft thrust of the bow.

The Todd party of five was shown to a spacious quilted-leather booth that could have accommodated ten. While the captain seated Sheila, Blixen watched the fiddlers, entranced. "Arthur," he said, "I applaud your taste. How did you find Aaron's?"

"They take American Express," Todd said. "They were first in the book."

"That's my old West Coast gourmet," Norm Seacliff said.

"Well, I asked Flanders if it was any good," Todd said, "and he told me it was, so if you don't like it, blame him."

"Oh, I hear it's very good," Flanders assured Seacliff.

Todd glanced at the waiting captain. "Anyway, who wants drinks? We all want drinks. Sheila?"

"Yes, I think I'll have scotch and Fresca," Sheila said.

"Jesus," Seacliff groaned.

"Scotch," the captain said, "and . . . ?"

"Fresca."

"Fresca. I'm not sure we have Fresca, madam."

"Oh. Well, Coke then."

"Plain Coca—"

"No, no, mixed with the scotch. Scotch and Coke."

The captain looked at his pad for a moment and then said: "I'd better see if we have any Coke," and left.

"One day," Seacliff said, "she's going to do this to a head waiter who'll insult her, and I'll feel obliged to fight him and I'll probably get terribly hurt."

"I think I'd better warn everybody," Sheila said, "that Mr. Seacliff is in one of his patented snits tonight."

"That's all I need," Todd said.

"Ignore her," Seacliff said. "I'm as sweet as ever I was."

"Listen," Sheila said, "you've been as mean as you could be to me all day long and I'm getting damn tired of it, too."

"Oh, for Pete's sake," Blixen said. "Look who's here."

"Where?" Todd asked, turning. "Who?"

"Isn't that Pablo Dooley?"

"By God, it is," Todd said.

"Two network presidents in one room?" Sheila said. "Heavens, I hope nobody throws a bomb, they'd cripple America's entertainment industry."

"Caution, sweetheart, caution," Seacliff said with a tender smile. "You're not going to be surrounded by guests forever. Sooner or later, we'll be alone again. Won't we?"

"Maybe," Sheila said, "and maybe not."

"He's coming over," Todd said. "You know Pablo, Norman . . ."

"Of course."

Pablo Dooley, spare and blond, an old man at thirty-five, approached them shaking his head and laughing. He pressed Todd's shoulder, bowed to Sheila, winked at Seacliff and Flanders, and gripped Blixen's hand. "Well, well, well," he said, "what have we here? A meeting of the supreme war council? How do we break through Dooley's blockbuster movies *next* season? How are you, Nils?"

"Pablo . . ."

"Let me give you a little well-meant advice, Nils. Demand a new time slot. We've got movies lined up for next year that'll make this year's ratings look sick. Right, Norman?"

"We'll see, we'll see," Seacliff said.

"I, myself, think you're whistling in the dark, boy," Todd said. "Did you catch the last Nielsens? The audience has begun to find us. One more swing around the circuit ought to put us right up in the top ten."

"Even you can't believe that, Arthur," Dooley said.

"I believe it."

"Ah, blissful ignorance. I ought to fill you in on some of our new titles."

"Fill away."

"And spoil your dinner?" Dooley laughed and sauntered off, waving.

"Damn smart-aleck," Todd muttered.

"I know what they've bought," Seacliff said, "and frankly it's second-rate."

"Yeah, but all the same . . ."

"Oh, *Lord,*" Sheila breathed behind her menu.

Blixen leaned to her sympathetically. "See anything you like there?"

"I was thinking of lobster. Then they'd bring me an apron and I could stuff it in my ears."

"Gets tiresome sometimes, shop talk."

"Well, it's just that that's all I hear, day in and day out. This program, that program, ratings, until I could scream. Why can't people in this industry ever talk about fashions, or bridge, or even fishing."

"Have you ever fished for grunion?" Blixen asked.

"What's a grunion?"

Todd, having evidently caught the word out of the corner of one ear, swung around to say: "Grunion's a seventeen-footer—"

"Seventeen-*footer!*" Sheila exclaimed. "My God, I'm scared of *trout!*"

"No, no," Blixen laughed. "He's talking about a boat. Aren't you?"

"Sure, sloop," Todd said. "Seventeen feet long, twenty-two-foot mast. Grunion. Sweet little craft. Why?"

"Well, we—"

The captain had returned and was poised behind Todd, waiting to interrupt. Blixen broke off.

"Mr. Blixen?" the captain addressed the table at large.

"Yes," Blixen said.

"Telephone call for you," said the captain. "This way . . ."

"Wait a minute," Todd burst out, "where's it from? Is it long distance?"

"It's from Mexico, I believe," the captain said.

Todd gestured at Flanders. "You go with him!"

"What?"

"Take your knife. If he tries anything funny, stab him in the back."

"What are you talking about, Arthur?" Seacliff demanded.

"Nothing. Flanders? Go on."

"I'm not about to run away, Arthur, for Christ's sake," Blixen said.

Seacliff put a hand on his arm. "This isn't apt to be bad news or anything, Nils, is it? Because I can't postpone the conference *or* the decision. It's tomorrow or it's never. Do you understand that?"

"Absolutely. Excuse me . . ."

"Uh—" Flanders said, "shall I . . . ?"

"No," Blixen said, "stay there. I'll be right back."

He was halfway to the vestibule, following the captain's tailored back, when he heard the footsteps behind him.

"I'm sorry," Flanders apologized. "He made me."

CHAPTER TWENTY-SEVEN

Schreiber's voice, when the bilingual operator's ultimately allowed it to come through, sounded breathy and intermittent. "The hotel gave me this number, Nils. Did I get you at a bad time?"

"Not at all. Any luck?"

"I'd say so, yes, a good deal. You were right about your man being well-known. He owns a *posada*—an inn. That's where I'm phoning from."

"You're sure you've got the right Morales?"

"Two-time lightweight champion of Mexico, fifty years old, five feet four inches tall, brown hair, brown eyes . . ."

"When was he last seen in Mazatlan?"

"I can see him in Mazatlan right now," Schreiber said. "He's standing next to me here."

Blixen sat down. Pressed between the short glass sides of the open telephone stall, he seemed aware of textures primarily—the soapy white feel of the phone in his hand, the scratch of tweed across his knee—as though everything had failed him for a moment but his sense of touch. The circular receiver was as cold as a seashell against his ear. Little by little he began to hear the pump of his own lungs, and then the enormously distant, hollow voice of Schreiber again, repeating his name. "Wade," he said, "would you wait just a second?" He carefully put down the phone and got his handkerchief out of his hip pocket and blew his nose. Flanders, looking wan and bedraggled, was pacing back and forth at the end of the bar with a drink in his hand. When he was certain of himself, Blixen put the handkerchief away and picked up the phone. "Hello?" he said.

"What happened?" Schreiber asked. "Were we cut off?"

"No. I thought I might have to sneeze." Blixen filled his lungs. "So. Rafael Morales is there with you."

"He's a little puzzled over what the purpose of our inquiry might be. I told him I was a little puzzled myself. Would you like to talk to him?"

"I certainly would," Blixen said.

"Here he is . . ."

The voice was soft and husky, as though the man had been punched too many times in the throat. "Hello, Mr. Blixen."

"Señor Morales," Blixen said, "I speak Spanish, if that would be easier for you."

"Not at all, sir, thank you. English will do."

"It's very good of you to give my friend and me this time."

"My pleasure."

"Mr. Morales—have you ever been to the United States?"

"No, I have not."

"Not even to southern California?"

"No."

"Yet you have some very close friends there."

After a pause, Morales said: "I'm not sure I understand what you mean."

"I was referring to Judith and Gloria Chavez."

Ghost voices chattered and bounced faintly along the line, but Morales remained silent.

"Do you recognize those names, Mr. Morales?"

"How close a friend are *you* to Gloria Chavez, Mr. Blixen?"

"Close enough to know how much the garnet ring you sent means to her. And to guess *why* it means so much."

"You know, it's a strange thing," Morales said. "I've been an inn-keeper for ten years, I've dealt with North Americans on a daily basis all that time—and I'm not yet used to North American directness. Probably I never will be."

"If I've offended you, I'm truly sorry. And I apologize."

"I can't decide whether I'm offended or not. I'm not even sure I have a right to be offended. A moralist might argue that I gave up that right twenty-five years ago, eh?"

"My God, who'd dare to be a moralist these days?" Blixen asked.

Morales laughed softly. "Maybe you're right."

"I'd like to ask you one or two more questions, Mr. Morales, if you wouldn't mind."

"Will they be as direct as the last one?"

"I'll try to be more discreet."

"Then go ahead."

"Have any of your friends visited southern California in the last few weeks?"

"No."

"Have you sent anyone at all up there with gifts—or a message?"

"No."

Blixen thought. "I'm going to describe a man to you. I'd like to know if this reminds you of anyone."

"All right."

"Fifty years old, brown hair worn long in the back, Mexican but with very little accent, short, affects an old flop-brimmed hat—"

"Of course."

Blixen sat up straighter. "You're acquainted with this man?"

"I'm acquainted with one very much like him. He's a salesman for a brewery in Leon. He stays here whenever he comes into town."

"When did you see him last?"

"Oh—ten days ago?"

"What's his name?"

"Herrero."

"Did *he* indicate he might be on his way to the States?"

"No. At least—well—it's funny you should mention my—mention Miss Chavez."

"Why?"

"Because," Morales said, "her name came up that night, too."

Blixen's palm had grown wet; he switched the phone to his other ear and wiped his hand on his trouser leg. "Can you tell me about it?"

There was a moment's silence. Then Morales said: "I—was talking about Gloria to a friend of mine, very old friend, who knew all about the girl and her mother—and me. It was very late. We were in the bar here, and I thought we were alone, but it seems Herrero was sitting in the shadows. I can't recall everything we said. My friend asked how Gloria was getting along and I remember telling him about the fine restaurant Jesus Mary had bought on the beach in Oceanport, and about Judith's back and one thing and another."

"How did you know about Judith's back?"

"We—keep in touch."

"Yes . . . what else?"

"That's about all. I wondered later how much Herrero had actually heard, because—well, I'm a married man, and . . . blackmailers can make life miserable sometimes."

"But Herrero didn't try to blackmail you?"

"He hasn't yet."

"I don't think he will," Blixen said.

"It wouldn't profit him in any case. The way to draw a backmailer's teeth is to admit the sin he expects you to hide. I made up my mind I'd tell my wife the minute he approached me."

"Much wiser," Blixen said, "than trying to eliminate him."

"Murder, you mean?" Morales sounded genuinely shocked. "But that's the act of a fool."

"Yes, it is." Blixen paused, considering his next question. Flanders had left the bar and was standing outside the next telephone stall, pushing the ice cubes in his drink around with the tip of his index finger. "Well, Mr. Morales," Blixen began, and then stopped, staring at Flanders.

"Yes, Mr. Blixen?" Morales said.

Numbly Blixen lowered the phone. "You're married," he said to Flanders.

Flanders gave a sheepish jump. "Married? Well—yes. Why? I mean—you knew that . . ."

"Oh, my God," Blixen whispered.

"Mr. Blixen?" cried the tiny voice in the telephone on his lap. "Mr. Blixen?"

Blixen squeezed his eyes shut, hearing the tumblers drop, seeing the puzzle nearly whole for the first time.

He felt Flanders's hand on his shoulder. "Nils, you sit right there. Take this drink. I'll see if I can find a doctor."

"I don't need a doctor! Do you have any change?"

"Do I have—?"

"For the phone, for the phone!"

"Oh. For the phone." Flanders's mouth had begun to tremble. "Well—yes. What phone?"

"Call the airport," Blixen said. "Find out when I can leave for L.A. The earliest possible—"

"Excuse me," Flanders began, but before he could move, Blixen's hand had clamped over his forearm. "Nils," Flanders moaned, "please, for God's sake, let me tell Arthur what's—"

Blixen's grip tightened. "Dwayne," he said softly, "are you going to do as I ask, or are we going to have a scene here?"

Flanders cast a wild-eyed look toward the dining room. "I guess I'm going to do as you ask."

"I don't care what the line is. I'll take any available flight."

"Oh, God . . ." Flanders fished change out of his pocket and crept into the neighboring stall like a galley slave into his shackles.

Blixen picked up his own receiver. "Mr. Morales—I want to thank you for all your help."

"*Have* I helped?"

"Very much."

"Well, I don't see how. But I'm glad. I think."

"Could I speak to Mr. Schreiber again?"

"Yes. He's right here. Goodbye, Mr. Blixen."

"Yes, Nils," Schreiber said.

"How far are you from the Mazatlan airport?"

"About twenty minutes."

"Call them as soon as I hang up, and charter a plane for Leon."

"Le—"

"Get the name of Herrero's brewery from Morales. Ask the people there for a full physical description of Herrero, pictures if there are any, fingerprints. I want to know when he last reported in."

"Where he is now?" Schreiber suggested.

"I know where he is now," Blixen said. "He's in the Ramona County morgue."

"The headless—"

"Hop to it, Wade, will you?"

"I will, but I don't understand what good fingerprints can do if you're thinking of establishing identification."

"Indulge me. What do you hear from Pep? About Junkin?"

"Pep flew to Montreal personally. He expects a break before noon tomorrow."

"Good. I'm coming home tonight. You can contact me tomorrow through DeGroot. Is everything clear?"

"Everything," Schreiber said, "except who killed Herrero, if it *is* Herrero, and why, and how you're able to leave New York so soon when I know you can't have had time to nail down the renewal."

"*Adios,* hombre, thanks," Blixen said, and rang off.

Flanders was still occupied in the next stall, scribbling figures on a scrap of paper and grunting: "Um hm, um hm," into the phone, so Blixen placed a long-distance call to DeGroot, who sounded ominously gentle when he came on.

"Well, well, well. Nils. I wondered if you'd remember little old me out here in the boondocks."

"First of all, did you drop the marijuana charge?"

"Oh, yes, we dropped it."

"How did Jesus react?"

"They all went back to the restaurant. They're there now, pow-wowing."

"So no one's left for Mexico?"

"Chavez hasn't."

"Good. All right—"

"Incidentally, I don't care who else leaves for Mexico," DeGroot said, "but if that bastard tries it, I might not even bother with the material-witness crap—just hit him with a Murder One."

"You're a hard man to help, Teet. Sometimes I despair for you."

"Well, you know us stubborn Dutchmen."

"Something tells me you've had another talk with Mrs. Junkin."

"Very psychic."

"And I'll just bet she's more certain than ever that it's her husband in the morgue."

"Ninety-nine and ninety-nine one-hundredths percent," DeGroot said.

"The man in the barrel," Blixen said, "was a beer salesman from Leon, Mexico, named Herrero."

After a long moment, DeGroot said: "How do you spell that?"

Blixen spelled it.

"You know I'll check with Missing Persons in Leon. Even you wouldn't be dumb enough to try a trick at this late date."

"No tricks."

"And you say this Herrero was a boxer?"

"Ah," Blixen said. "Well. I was a bit off target on that one, Teet. No. He wasn't a boxer—he was a blackmailer."

"Who killed him?"

"I'll tell you tomorrow."

"You'll tell me now."

"I haven't got all the pieces yet."

"So you're really not sure."

"Ninety-nine and ninety-nine one-hundredths percent," Blixen said. "No more. All I know for certain is that Jesus Mary didn't do it."

He could hear the creak of DeGroot's chair and the slap of a pencil thrown down on the desk. "Not good enough," DeGroot said.

Uneasily Blixen leaned forward. "What do you mean not—"

"Maybe the dead man's Junkin, maybe it's this Herrero, but whoever it is, the body was found on Chavez's property, and Chavez is part of it. I've got my material-witness warrant. I'm going to serve him."

"Teet, for Christ's sake," Blixen exploded, "don't you listen to a word I say?"

"Not when you say Chavez is innocent."

"Will you use your head! Trout had to have been murdered by whoever killed Herrero! They wanted you to go on thinking Herrero was Junkin! That's why they stole the X rays! Now, you saw Trout alive at two-thirty. But six men and a bartender alibi Jesus Mary solidly between two and *four*-thirty. He couldn't possibly—"

"Who says Trout was murdered?"

"Of course he was murdered!"

"The room was locked," DeGroot said, "the—"

"Do you mean to sit there and tell me you haven't figured that one out yet? What have you—!" Blixen snapped his mouth shut and forced himself to breathe deeply and evenly. "Teet," he said, "I asked you before about Trout's autopsy. Do you have those results?"

"Yes."

"And Trout had been heavily sedated, hadn't he?"

In the adjoining stall, Flanders hung up and sat slumped on the chair, rereading his notes.

"Well," DeGroot muttered, "I don't see that that proves—"

"Excuse me a minute," Blixen broke in. He leaned back and around the side of the stall. "Dwayne?"

"You won't like it," Flanders said hopelessly. "Why don't you wait until—"

"I said any flight."

Flanders appeared ready to weep. "Well, the only thing out of here before midnight is a semischeduled milk-run on Atlantis that leaves Kennedy at ten, stops twice, and gets into L.A. International at eight in the morning."

"What's Atlantis?"

"No idea in the world."

Blixen hesitated, then returned to his phone. "Teet? I've got to catch a plane at Kennedy, but I swear I'll explain everything to you tomorrow. In the meantime, please don't push Chavez into a corner neither one of you can squirm out of. Give me until noon. If I haven't shown you by then who really killed Herrero and Trout—"

"Tread water until you whistle, is that it?"

Blixen glanced around. The adjacent stall was empty; he swiveled his head in time to see Flanders's broad back disappearing into the dining room.

"I don't like this a damn bit," DeGroot said.

Blixen wiped the corner of his mouth, waiting.

"Until when?" DeGroot asked.

"Noon."

"Do you know what's going to happen if you poop out on me this time, Nils?"

"I know," Blixen said.

"One more game, then," DeGroot said. *"One* more."

"Teet, you won't regret it," Blixen said. He blew his breath out sharply. "Now, there are a couple of things you can do for me. Would you ask Sanderson to pick me up at L.A. International at eight tomorrow morning? I'll be on Atlantis. And I'll want a copy of Wednesday's L.A. *Times.*"

Curiosity overcame truculence. *"Wednes*day's?"

"If he can't find the whole thing, tell him all I'll need is the national weather news page."

"Why?"

In the vestibule archway, Norm Seacliff's bald head bobbed toward the stalls like a heavy balloon.

Blixen crouched closer to the phone. "Next—do you have a copy of the autopsy report on the man in the barrel?"

"Not here in the office."

"Then call the coroner and ask him what part of the body was amputated first—left hand, right hand, or head."

"Nils—"

"It's important, Teet. I wouldn't ask if it wasn't important."

"Coroner," DeGroot muttered. "Left hand, right hand, head—"

"I'll see you at nine tomorrow morning." Blixen hung up the phone, contemplated it for a moment, then rose and turned.

Seacliff had stopped behind him. His thick-striped tie had twisted rakishly to the left; he had lowered his head to look at Blixen out of the bloodshot tops of his eyes. "Well, Nils?" he asked softly.

"Well, Norman," Blixen replied, "I'm sorry it couldn't have worked out."

"That idiot child was telling the truth, then," Seacliff said. "Arthur didn't believe him. I thought I'd better check for myself."

Blixen glanced at his watch. "I'll have to leave. I'm going to be cutting it pretty close. I'm sorry I can't have a final drink with you."

"I'm not," Seacliff said.

Blixen raised his eyebrows, shrugged, and started away.

"Nils," Seacliff said. "You did grasp what I was saying in there earlier? It's over, you know."

"Yes. I know."

"You have a goddamn funny set of values, my friend."

Blixen shook his head. "Just a different set, Norman," he said.

CHAPTER TWENTY-EIGHT

Los Angeles lay like a doomed dragon in a tar pit, strangling on its own fire and smoke. By eight in the morning the filthy air was unfit to breathe; Sanderson met him at the gate with a handkerchief pressed to his streaming eyes. "The most courageous men in America," he said, "have got to be the pilots who can steel themselves to dive out of all that fresh air into this soup. How was your flight?"

"The only things we lacked," Blixen said, "were goggles and a long white scarf."

"Old airplane?"

"Not for a Jenny."

He never had been so tired. All the tortuous way home, he had fallen into one fitful doze after another, only to pop awake with the conviction that he must be wrong, that he had left something out of the equation, that the murderer couldn't possibly be the one he knew it was. "Did you bring Wednesday's *Times?*"

"It's in the car."

They retrieved his battered overnight bag and made their way across the airport street to the parking lot.

"Oh—" Sanderson said, "apparently you wanted to know what part of the victim was chopped off first?"

"Yes."

"DeGroot said to tell you it was the right hand."

"No question about that?"

"Not from the report he read me. It had to do with hesitation marks on the wrist and the look of the severed arteries and so forth. The right hand was first—a bad job—then the head—then the left hand."

The ramshackle Cadillac groaned under their weight.

"I told Teet I'd see him at nine," Blixen said. "Can we make it?"

"I think so. He's in Oceanport, at the restaurant. He asked me to bring you there."

Wednesday's *Times* lay on the seat between them. Blixen opened it to the weather page.

"I . . . notice you haven't said anything about our renewal," Sanderson said. "Is no news good news in this case? Or—"

"Not in this case."

Sanderson whistled, gazing straight ahead. "Pity," he said.

Blixen closed the paper, saddened, certain, and sat gazing at his hands while the car bounced and sped toward the freeway. "One more thing," he said. "What was the cause of death? Were they ever able to pin that down for sure?"

"Well, this is really weird," Sanderson said. "He was drowned."

"Seawater in the lungs?"

"No. Fresh."

Blixen nodded.

The freeway swallowed them.

"Nils," Sanderson said, "what's this all about? What does all this mean—the right hand, the newspaper . . . ?"

But there was no answer, and when Sanderson glanced over, he saw that Blixen was already asleep.

CHAPTER TWENTY-NINE

The sky over Oceanport was pearl-colored and low when Blixen woke; gulls cried and wheeled past the restaurant. DeGroot stood beside the first barricade, waiting for them.

"What day is this?" Blixen asked.

"This is Friday," Sanderson answered. "Why?"

"You called me at Arthur's last Monday night. Can you believe that?"

"Time really flies when you're having fun, doesn't it," Sanderson said.

DeGroot waved them to a stop and then stumped around the front of the car to open Blixen's door. "You're late," he said. "It's two minutes past nine. If you can't be punctual, don't make dates."

"You're in a merry mood," Blixen said.

"Just fatigue."

"Did you contact Leon?"

"I did. Juan Herrero was last heard from in Tijuana when he phoned the brewery to advise them he was heading north for the weekend. He said if anybody absolutely needed him, he could be reached at the Cucaracha Restaurant in Oceanport."

Blixen looked across at the warped, graffiti-scarred building. "Was Herrero married?"

"No."

"Any family at all?"

"No."

"Thank God for small mercies."

"Incidentally," DeGroot said, "I heard from your attorney."

"And?"

"He said he was forwarding Herrero's photograph and right thumb print. The brewery keeps an employee-identification file."

"Good. Good."

"He also told me that Pep Cisneros had located Junkin."

"Junkin!" exclaimed Sanderson. "Where?"

Evenly, still concentrating on Blixen, DeGroot said: "Montreal. Mrs. Junkin has already talked to him. He intends to stay. He's living in a basement with three young hippie girls and a black militant named Jomo. He told Mrs. Junkin that if she came after him, he'd swarm all over her."

After a moment Blixen said: "So you won't need a deposition. Mrs. Junkin's satisfied he's alive?"

" 'Satisfied' is a strange way to put it, but yes," DeGroot said. "At least that's one mystery cleared up."

The restaurant door slammed; Isabel, in a white turtleneck sweater, suede skirt and knee socks, came striding purposefully toward them across the sidewalk and the pitted street.

"Hell," DeGroot muttered. "Well, there goes my peaceful morning."

"Watch it, friend," Sanderson growled.

Isabel clumped to a stop in front of Blixen, threw her hair back. "I saw you out the window. Hello, *patrón*."

"Hello, *ahijada*."

"Welcome back."

"Thank you."

"I'm stalling a little bit here. I've got something to say and I don't quite know how to approach it."

"Just start," Sanderson said.

Isabel looked at him and then gave a brisk nod. "Okay, *patrón*, I've been mulling over your airport lecture, and I've come to a shocking conclusion." She tried to shove her hands into pockets that weren't there and settled for gripping them in front of her. "I think you were right."

"I'm glad, *ahijada*."

"Odd. The minute I took the world off my back, I felt strong enough to act and fight both."

"That's often the way of it."

Isabel jerked her head over her left shoulder. "They're packing in there. Jude's back feels better. She and Jesus Mary are returning to Mazatlan."

"*Are* they now," DeGroot said. "Well, by God, we'll see about *that*."

Ignoring him, Isabel said: "They invited me to come along. I said no. I told them I had a series to film."

Blixen took her chin in his hand, tilted her face upward, and kissed her on the forehead.

Isabel moved into his arms and pressed her head against his shoulder. "By God," she mumbled, "we may never win an Emmy, but we'll give 'em a show we're proud of, right?"

"Right," Blixen said.

"Babe," Sanderson said, then stopped.

"What?" When he failed to answer, Isabel raised her eyes. Sanderson was frowning at the seawall. "Well? What?"

"We lost the show, babe," Sanderson said.

At last Isabel stepped away from Blixen.

"Isabel," Blixen said, "what's that on your back?"

But she wouldn't look at him. She bit her upper lip, regarding the restaurant cryptically.

"Whose fault was it, Isabel?" Blixen asked.

"Not mine . . ." But it was nearly a question.

"Mine, if anybody's," Blixen said, "because of the priorities I gave it. Or didn't give it. But not mine, either. This show had become a chunk of meat to throw to a dog named Connaught, to stop his barking."

Isabel swung her head around. "Connaught's the one who's such a nut on violence."

"That's right."

"But there isn't any violence on our show."

"That doesn't matter. The time slot was wrong. The ratings were bad. Better to placate Connaught by killing *Stagg* than to let him keep blundering around. He might have lit out after a successful series. The network has its reasons, which reason knows nothing of. Embroider that on your next pillow."

The uncertainty in her eyes cleared little by little. "Not my fault," she muttered. "I know that."

"Are you sure of it?"

She straightened. "Yes."

"We'll do a new one next year," Blixen said, "if you'll work with me again."

"They don't call me Pushover Chavez for nothing. All you have to do is whistle."

Blixen grinned.

"In the meantime," DeGroot said, "we've still got a murder to clear up."

"Two murders," Blixen said. He nodded toward the restaurant. "Are they all over there now?"

"The whole family," Isabel said.

"Anybody else?"

"Brouwer."

Blixen slapped the folded newspaper against his leg. "All right, let's see if we can cut this Gordian knot."

"*Patrón*," Isabel said. She touched his arm uneasily. "I—think I finally figured something else out, too. I'm slow but I'm persistent. When you were asking me about Rafael Morales—" She hesitated.

"Yes?"

"Well. I remembered later that Gloria's middle name is Rafaela. *Patrón*, she *isn't* like Jesus Mary. . . ."

"No, she isn't."

"And—Morales would be about fifty now. And the man in the barrel was about fifty."

"It isn't Morales," Blixen said.

"How do you know?"

"I talked to him. He owns an inn in Mazatlan."

"Talked to him about—Jesus Mary, and Jude, and Gloria?"

"Yes."

Isabel fell silent for a time. Then: "Will all this have to come out when you discuss the case with them?"

"I don't think so."

Gravely grateful, Isabel nodded. "I wonder if Jesus Mary was *my* father . . ."

"No," Blixen said. "He wasn't."

Isabel's musing eyes sought his. "You sound pretty positive."

"I am."

Presently Isabel made a wry face. "I'd better not ask why. You can't take *all* a man's *machismo* away from him."

"Maybe *machismo*'s a little higher than most men think," Blixen said. "Perhaps around the heart."

Smiling, Isabel murmured: "Perhaps." She turned. "Well . . ."

"Now, he's going to raise a lot of hell," DeGroot said, "when I show up over there."

"I'll handle it," Isabel said. "I'm not afraid of him anymore." She glanced at Blixen. "I love him, and that's better than fear any day anyway, isn't it?"

"Much better," Blixen said.

CHAPTER THIRTY

The tiny top-floor room was crowded and loud. Gloria and Cabral appeared to be arguing with Brouwer by the window; Judith, dressed for traveling, stood gingerly near the closet, trying to choose a hat from a selection in Mrs. Billroth's arms; Jesus Mary, hefting the black-thorn cane in one hand, uttered a grunt of anger and surprise when he saw DeGroot.

Judy followed his gaze. "Mr. Blixen!"

Grimly Jesus Mary pushed past her to point the cane at DeGroot. "*You!*" he roared, and motioned the cane toward the door. "Out!"

"Tio," Isabel began.

"Tio nothing! This is still my property! And I want that bloody Cossack off it!"

"He'll get off it," Isabel snapped, "when he's finished his business here. Now sit down and be quiet."

Incredulously, Jesus Mary began to suck air into his lungs.

"Sit down, tio! Before you burst like a balloon."

Jesus Mary closed his mouth, opened it again, closed it again, and sat down on the bed.

Cabral hit the side of his head to clear it and stared in disbelief at Jesus Mary.

"Chu-Chu, are you all right?" Judith asked in a wavery voice. But Jesus Mary remained mute and Judith, at a loss, turned rigidly to the sheriff. "If you think you're going to arrest him for Junkin's murder—"

"Nobody's going to try," DeGroot said.

Cabral stuck out his jaw. "Or on any other super-patriotic red-baiting—"

"Ray," Gloria interrupted, "wait a minute." Deliberately she moved to DeGroot, stood looking up at him. "What *are* you here for, Sheriff?"

"To arrest the murderer of Juan Herrero," DeGroot said.

Judith lowered herself onto a tufted bench. Cabral said something to Gloria in a low voice.

"Who's Juan Herrero?" Mrs. Billroth asked.

DeGroot shot her a piercing glance. The room was utterly still for five endless seconds. Then DeGroot said lamely: "I think I'll just let Mr. Blixen answer that."

Every eye went to Blixen, who had been watching one face for reactions, and who had seen what he'd been seeking. "Juan Herrero," he said slowly, "was a blackmailer who tried to practice his trade in the wrong place and ended up dead for his trouble."

"Excuse me, Mr. Blixen," Brouwer said, "but was Herrero the man who came to my church?"

Cabral frowned. "Came to your church when?"

"Last Saturday. I was alone, and this man—Herrero—dropped in to ask me some questions about the Cucaracha, and so I sent him up to see Jesus Mary."

Gloria's face was perplexed. "But I don't remember anyone coming in at all that night. Daddy, you didn't say anything about it."

"No one *did* come in," Jesus Mary whispered.

"And yet someone here saw Herrero Saturday night," Blixen said, "and killed him."

"Someone *here?*" Mrs. Billroth cried.

"Oh, yes."

"I don't believe it," Brouwer said. "Someone *in this room* killed a perfect stranger, then cut off his head and his hands?"

"But he wasn't a stranger," Blixen said. "Dr. Trout, for one, had seen him before, probably had treated him, probably could have tied him in with the murderer as soon as he saw the corpse. So Dr. Trout had to be killed."

"Trout killed himself," Cabral declared in a belligerent tenor.

Blixen shook his head. "No." His glance swept the bedroom baseboard, fastened on a gas nipple and turncock. "All of the buildings along this street were designed to accommodate room heaters, I imagine. Do you have one?"

Judith stirred. "A heater? In the closet."

Curiously Cabral retrieved the heater, stood looking from it to Blixen and back again.

"Let's see if it works," Blixen said. He placed the heater on the floor near the outlet, attached the end of the green hose to the nipple, struck a match, opened the turncock. The gas caught, flared feebly.

"It's probably clogged," Isabel said.

"It'll do." Blixen straightened. "Trout was found on the couch in his sitting room with a drink on the floor beside him, the gas on, and his room locked."

DeGroot cleared his throat. "I think I ought to tell you that there were prints on that turncock, Nils. And they were Trout's."

"I'm sure they were Trout's. He turned the gas on."

"Well, what are you trying to say?" Brouwer put in. "That this mysterious murderer somehow hypnotized him into suicide?"

"Not at all. Unless a strong sedative counts as a hypnotic," Blixen considered. "Picture the scene. The murderer stands talking casually to Trout while the sedative takes effect. Trout can't understand why he's so sleepy. Maybe it's the warmth of the room; the gas is lit. The murderer suggests that Trout lock the door and lie down for a second, that it's probably the unaccustomed drink in the afternoon. Trout agrees and the murderer goes." Blixen illustrated his words by crossing to the door. "The murderer leaves and Trout, too sleepy to react, is doomed."

"*Why?*" Mrs. Billroth asked. "I don't understand."

"Look at the heater," Blixen said.

The flames were out. Gas hissed gently into the room. Cabral jumped to the outlet, closed the turncock.

"What *happened?*" Judith cried.

"I stepped on the hose," Blixen said. "They're old, all these hoses, they're easily pinched. The flame was killed. When I released my foot, the gas was free to flow into the room. Simplest trick in the world. I would have thought anyone could spot it."

"All right," DeGroot growled, "let's talk about opportunity."

"Let's do that," Blixen agreed. "The trick was performed some time around two-thirty, probably minutes after the sheriff left. Where was everyone at two-thirty?" He turned. "Mr. Chavez?"

"In a bar," Jesus Mary said.

"Mrs. Billroth?"

"Sailing."

"Gloria?"

"Up here—all afternoon—with my mother."

"Mr. Cabral?"

"Two-thirty?" Cabral thought. "I was driving back from Baja, with a chaplain friend of mine."

"Yes," Blixen said. He looked at Brouwer. "Alfred?"

Brouwer rotated the coonskin cap between his hands. "I was writing a sermon."

"In your church?"

"Yes."

"Alone?"

"Yes."

"But we saw him, you know," Mrs. Billroth said. "He was in his window. We called to him—"

"Did he answer?"

"I didn't hear them," Brouwer said.

"Too absorbed?"

"Yes."

"Wait a minute," Cabral said. He had hooked his thumbs under his belt and was bent forward, staring at Brouwer.

Blixen glanced at him. "Yes, Mr. Cabral?"

"I just thought of something."

"And what was that?"

"He was alone on Saturday night, too."

"So he was," Blixen murmured.

Confused, Brouwer said: "Well—what does that have to do with Trout's death? Just because—"

"Not Trout, dear," Mrs. Billroth said slowly. "I think they're saying that you were the last one to see poor Mr. Herrero alive." She blinked at Blixen. "Aren't you?"

CHAPTER THIRTY-ONE

The cooling heater clicked in the still room.

Suddenly Brouwer gave an explosive laugh. "You're not serious!" he said. "You *can't* be serious! Why in the world would I want to harm a man I'd never set eyes on in my life?"

"Suppose you tell us, son," DeGroot said.

"I *can't* tell you! Because I didn't do it!" Brouwer spun to Blixen. "He came in, he asked me if the restaurant was open—and I sent him on. That's exactly what happened! That's *all* that happened!"

"I know it is," Blixen said.

Brouwer stared. "Then—you believe me?"

"Of course."

"Well, why don't you believe me when I say I was writing a sermon at two-thirty?"

"I do," Blixen said.

Isabel had found a pencil somewhere and was scratching her head through the thick hair above her left ear. "Nils," she said.

Impatiently DeGroot said: "Let me hop in first for a minute here." He ran a hand over his face. "If *Brouwer* has an alibi, then that accounts for everybody. Why did you say the murderer was in this room? There's nobody left—"

"There's you," Jesus Mary said.

Brouwer burst out with another of his unhinged laughs. "Mother of God!" he said. "What next?"

"Well?" Jesus Mary looked at Blixen.

"Well what?"

"I could make a pretty good case against him."

"You'd be wrong," Blixen said.

"Listen," Judith said, "I think this has gone on just about long enough. You may think it's funny—"

"Oh, no," Blixen said, "I don't think it's funny at all. And I agree with you. It's gone on much too long." He turned his head. "Well, Enid?" he asked. "Shall we end it?"

Mrs. Billroth, as colorful as a street peddler with her arms full of hats, continued to look at Jesus Mary, smiling faintly.

"Enid?" Blixen repeated quietly.

"What?"

"They're sending a thumbprint of Herrero's. They'll find his hands sooner or later. Mr. DeGroot's going to take you to Ramona City now. Are you ready?"

"Who's ever ready?" Mrs. Billroth asked. "I'm terribly tired, though, I'll tell you that." She let her head droop a little. "I don't believe I've ever been so tired," she said.

Isabel started toward her, but DeGroot held out his arm and Isabel halted.

In a voice sick with pain, Judith said to no one in particular: *"Enid?"*

"Translate 'Juan Herrero' for me," Blixen requested.

" 'John Smith.' "

"Let's call him John Smith for a minute," Blixen said. "He wasn't a Mexican, although he'd lived there for twenty years. And he wasn't looking for the Cucaracha Restaurant. He was looking for the woman who'd sold it. He thought he deserved a share of the profit. He was the woman's husband."

"No, you're wrong," Cabral insisted. "Larry Billroth had a heart attack and died twenty years ago."

"He had a heart attack," Blixen agreed, "but he didn't die. He may have come close to it, and that may have given him his idea. His marriage, like George Junkin's, was an unsatisfactory one. He might have been approaching the end of his life, like Junkin, without ever having really lived it. So he proposed a scheme to Enid and to their best friend, Dr. Harold Trout. He *would* die. Trout would sign the death certificate, Enid would inherit enough life insurance to buy the tea shop she'd always wanted, and Billroth himself would disappear into Mexico."

"But there was an autopsy," Cabral said. "I can remember something about that. . . ."

"Trout told me once he'd been a coroner," Blixen said. "Who was coroner in Ramona County then?"

"Trout was," DeGroot breathed. "So the autopsy report was false, too. But—they must have buried *some*one."

"A hobo, perhaps. A drowned man with no identification. A suicide . . ." Blixen glanced at Mrs. Billroth. "In any event, twenty years pass. South of the border, Larry Billroth lives a completely unpressured life, fiddling when he wants to instead of when he has to, traveling, growing stronger—and poorer—every day. Time and again he wonders how Enid has made out with the insurance. He imagines that she's pyramided the money into two shops, a chain of shops. But he doesn't dare go back to see. Until one night in Mazatlan, in a *posada,* when he happens to overhear two men talking about the Cucaracha Restaurant in Oceanport. He hears them say that Jesus Mary Chavez has bought the business from Mrs. Enid Billroth."

"Who were these men?" Jesus Mary asked quietly. "How did they know about me? It's been years since I wrote to anyone in Mazatlan."

"But *I* write," Judy said. Her face was pale; she gazed straight at Blixen. "I have dozens of friends there. The Quinones. The Guzmans. Padre Sor. One of them must have been at the *posada.*"

"So it would seem," Blixen said.

"But which one?" Jesus Mary persisted.

"What does it matter, tio?" Isabel broke in. "Let him get on with the telling."

Slowly Jesus Mary looked from his niece to his daughter to his wife. Judy's eyes remained on Blixen. Gloria, her back turned, stood at the window. At last Jesus Mary rested his face in his hands. "You're right," he said wearily. "It doesn't matter."

"In effect, then," Brouwer said to Blixen, "Billroth got greedy. Is that what happened?"

"Is it, Enid?" Blixen asked.

It was as though the words were pleasant but nearly meaningless to her at first, like English spoken in a lilting brogue. She gazed at Blixen's lips, puzzled. "Ah. Yes, yes. He thought I'd made a fortune, you see."

"Where did he find you Saturday night?" Blixen asked.

"Right here," said Mrs. Billroth, smiling and nodding amiably. "At the counter. Having some chili. Well, you can imagine how surprised I was. He'd aged—but I recognized him. I took his arm and hustled him right off to my apartment."

"But not, I think, before someone saw you."

Again Mrs. Billroth brightened. "Dear, I don't like you at all, but you are clever. Yes. Isabel saw us at the front door. She came in from the kitchen just as we were leaving."

"But I didn't see a thing," Isabel protested. "I had a terrible headache—blind headache."

"Well, I didn't know that, did I," explained Mrs. Billroth reasonably. "I assumed you'd certainly seen Larry, and that you'd tell the whole world about it, a case of the tongue wagging the girl."

"Which is why you tried to run her down that night," Blixen suggested.

"Yes."

"Where did you get the strychnine?"

"Harold gave me that strychnine years and years ago. For the rats. When I saw how much was left, I thought right away of using it on Isabel. She was the one who suggested the sugar substitute. She asked me for my bottle, so I gave it to her. With the strychnine." Mrs. Billroth's ugly face fell. "I can't tell you how upset I was when Harpo got it instead. I cannot bear to see a dog suffer. What a useless, useless death . . . I didn't want anything like that to happen again, so I took the strychnine out and buried it and put the sugar substitute back."

"Then that was you in the fog," Isabel said.

"That was I."

DeGroot cleared his throat. "My deputy reported that you came down from upstairs when you heard the commotion in the alley."

"Oh, yes, that's true," said Mrs. Billroth. "Judith was asleep when Isabel left—she'd taken a sedative—so I popped down the outside staircase and followed Isabel. She circled back to the alley, back to the apartment. I picked up one of Junkin's little crowbars and I hit her. Then I slipped past Mr. Sanderson to the restaurant and returned up the outside staircase. Judith was still asleep. I went down the back stairs this time and asked the young deputy what all the yelling was about."

"But you were alone with me a couple of times after that," Isabel said, "and you didn't try anything."

"She found out that night about your blind headaches," Blixen reminded Isabel. "There was no more need to fear what you'd seen. Obviously you hadn't seen anything at all."

"It's Harpo I regret," said Mrs. Billroth. "I think it was very wicked of you to give him all that coffee, Isabel. You should have been more careful."

"Enid!" Isabel began, and then threw up her hands. "Forget it, forget it."

"Yes, least sewed, soonest mended," said Mrs. Billroth. But they could tell that she was still resentful.

"Enid," Blixen said, "can we get back to your husband for a moment."

"Oh, I suppose so."

"You took him to your apartment . . ."

"Yes."

"Gave him a drink with a sedative in it?"

"Yes. He wanted to take a bath while we talked. When he got sleepy, I drowned him. I hated to do it. It was like killing part of myself. But I couldn't let him pull me down into his own hell, could I?"

" 'For it is profitable for thee,' " Brouwer quoted half to himself, " 'that one of thy members should perish and not that thy whole body should be cast into hell.' "

"But why in the name of heaven," Cabral put in, "did you cut off his hands and his head?"

But Mrs. Billroth's attention had drifted; her complexion was poor and she seemed extremely tired.

"She cut off the right hand," Blixen explained, "because she couldn't remove Billroth's big wedding ring. She planned to bury the body and she didn't want anything left that could identify it. The ring probably bore both their names."

"*Wedding* ring?" DeGroot questioned. "On the *right* hand? Who wears wedding rings on the right?"

Blixen turned slightly. "Cabral?" he murmured.

Cabral was nodding. "Yes. Violinists often do. String players. Especially big rings. Because they might ball up the fingering."

"I began to put two and two together," Blixen said, "when I noticed that a young coworker of mine in New York wore a wedding ring on his left hand, naturally—but that the professional violinists who were playing in the next room had *their* rings on their right hands. I remembered how the rings had flashed every time their bows had moved."

"That's one hand," Isabel said. "Why the head?"

"Look at Cabral's throat," Blixen directed. "Left side—just under the jaw."

Obligingly, Cabral lifted his head for them to see. The dark, quarter-sized callus made by the constant pressure of the violin butt stood out like a burn. "Every violinist has this," Cabral said. "Can't be avoided."

"And again," Blixen said, "it's a mark that would have identified Billroth's profession. So the head went. The left hand followed when Enid realized that the tips of those fingers, too, were calloused."

"Where did all this absentminded butchery take place?" DeGroot wanted to know.

"I imagine in the bathtub," Blixen replied. "I'd have your lab men check the drain. She'll tell you eventually what she did with the head and the hands. I have a hunch she kept them in her apartment until Isabel and Gloria decided to move over, and then threw them in one of the canyons."

"Why didn't she do that with the body?"

"I'm sure she thought of it. She found a mover's barrel in Junkin's alley, stuffed the corpse into it—and then must have been unable to lift it into her car. So she borrowed Junkin's tilt-back dolly—it's still out there—and she trundled the barrel to the restaurant shed."

"Again, why?" DeGroot demanded.

"What better place could there be? It would look like just one more in the series of outrages that Jesus Mary and his family were living through. I'd guess she put it there early Sunday morning. Then she tried to alibi herself with Judith by pretending to hear noises out back on Monday night. Judith went along willingly enough. It was easy to imagine noises that night."

There was a momentary silence. Mrs. Billroth sat contentedly on the bed, half listening.

"Nils," Sanderson asked, "are you ready to tell us yet about the newspaper?"

"Well, obviously," Blixen said, "it wasn't the weather report I was interested in. It was the tide table."

"Oh, obviously," Sanderson said.

"When I was talking to Alfred Tuesday night on the bridge outside his church, he said something that didn't make any sense to me."

"Yes, you mentioned that," Brouwer said. "Did you remember what it was?"

"Finally. You stated that it was a twenty-five-foot drop from the bridge to the water."

"And so it is."

"Yet I can judge depths at that distance almost to the inch, and I could have sworn that the drop was less than twenty feet."

"You must be wrong."

Blixen shook his head. "The official measurement had to have been made at low tide. That night there was a full moon. The tide at nine o'clock was high." He glanced at Cabral. "What's the spread here, Cabral?"

"From low to high tide? A little over five feet."

"And in hours?"

"Slightly less than six."

"So that Wednesday's low tide would have occurred around quarter to three in the afternoon?"

"Yes."

"Question," Blixen said. "How does a sloop with a twenty-two-foot mast squeeze under a bridge less than twenty-five feet above the water?"

Sanderson stiffened, looked at Isabel, and then back at Blixen. "Well, it did. So it can. I suppose we went up the estuary while the tide was still going out."

"You'd have had to do it when the tide was at its lowest possible point," Blixen said.

Bewildered, Isabel said: "Listen, I'm pretty dumb when it comes to mathematics, but I don't believe I'm *that* dumb. What am I missing? We didn't clear the bridge by much, but we had around six inches. Say the distance up to the bridge at that time was twenty-three feet. With a twenty-two-foot mast, we'd *still* have a foot left. Wouldn't we?"

"Would you, David?" Blixen asked.

Sanderson's face was grim. "No," he said.

Isabel spun to him. "Why not?"

"Because the mast is measured from the deck," Sanderson said. "From the deck to the water is another two and a half feet at least. Therefore the Grunion mast rises at least twenty-four and a half feet." He bowed to Blixen. "You're right. We were at absolute low tide—or we couldn't have cleared it."

"And absolute low tide occurred," Blixen said, "according to the L.A. *Times* table, at two forty-eight Wednesday afternoon."

"Two forty-*eight!*" Isabel exclaimed. "No! We were there between twenty and twenty-five minutes past two!"

"You couldn't have been," Blixen said.

"But—!"

"Babe, don't you see it?" Sanderson asked. "She'd set my watch back half an hour. She went upstairs when you were dressing, killed Trout at two-thirty, showed you my watch, which said two, and drove you down to the marina. *I* didn't have another watch. I couldn't have told that you were half an hour late." He rubbed his forehead. "Then I imagine she set the watch forward again sometime during the sail. Neither of us would have noticed."

DeGroot sighed. "All right, Mrs. Billroth, will you come with me, please?"

The others watched in silence as Mrs. Billroth rose and crossed to the door with DeGroot. At the last moment she stopped in front of Blixen, put her two hands over his, and gave them a fond press. "It's not nice to hate," she said, "but I really just can't stand you." She twinkled up at him. "*You're* the one I should have killed," she said.

EPILOGUE

Nothing in the canyon was more outraged than he was.

He was upside down in someone's hands, being waved. He caught a gyrating glimpse of a sheriff's uniform, tangled Dutch eyebrows. "Look at this, Nils. How old do you suppose this wrinkled bastard is?"

"No date carved on him?"

"Nope."

"I suppose he could be a hundred."

"I'll bet he never saw anything like that sack before. I wonder what he thought when it came rolling down here?"

"I can tell you what he thought. He thought, well, for Christ's sake, what now? The same thing I thought when Arthur called."

"I'm glad they changed their minds about the series."

"Seacliff didn't change *his* mind. Pablo Dooley picked it up. For another network."

"Well, it'll be on the air. That's what counts, isn't it?"

"That, indeed, is what counts. . . ."

The violent hands set him down; the conversation diminished as the men climbed the hill.

He was alone again, already poised on the brink of sleep.

He wondered when the birds would drop him another berry. . . .

A.